DARK MOON

KISS OF DEATH

Other thrillers
you will enjoy:

The Mummy
by Barbara Steiner

The Phantom
by Barbara Steiner

Silent Witness
by Carol Ellis

Twins
by Caroline B. Cooney

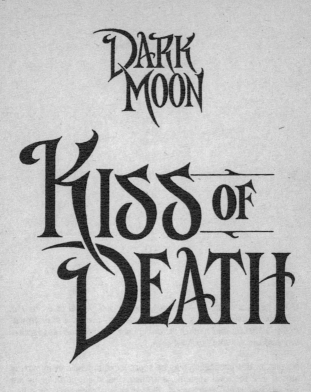

DARK MOON

KISS OF DEATH

ELIZABETH MOORE

SCHOLASTIC INC.
New York Toronto London Auckland Sydney

ISBN 0-590-25509-6

Copyright © 1995 by Dona Smith.
All rights reserved. Published by Scholastic Inc.

12 11 10 9 8 7 6 5 4 3 2   5 6 7 8 9/9 0/0

Printed in the U.S.A.   01

First Scholastic printing, June 1995

Chapter 1

It was just after midday. A thick blanket of humidity pressed in on the seaside resort town of Winthrop, Massachusetts. The sun scorched the streets, making them shimmer with a silvery haze. The few who ventured limply out of their houses wilted in the heat.

All at once, the silence deepened. An unearthly calm settled over the town.

Then (strange, there wasn't any noise to warn that it was coming) out of nowhere a long fire-red convertible rocketed down the street. It's nail-lacquer finish shone. The chrome glistened in the sun.

The girl who drove the car was radiant, glowing as if lit by a flame from within. Her black hair billowed out behind her in an ebony cloud. At her throat was a black velvet choker with a single bloodred jewel in the center.

In front of Abbott's grocery store and news-

stand, elderly Mrs. Ada Cary sensed something in the air before the car approached and
she stood perfectly still. Six-year-old Tony
Thomas stopped kicking stones. A prickle of
excitement made Mr. Abbott stop what he was
doing and come outside. They all felt as if they
were . . . waiting.

The three people on the sidewalk stared in
astonishment as the gleaming red machine
flashed into view. As the car went speeding
by they caught a glimpse of the girl behind the
wheel, and their expressions changed from
amazed to awestruck.

Of course, each of them could see the girl
was beautiful. They could recognize beautiful
hair, beautiful skin, beautiful eyes. The girl had
all of that — and more. She had something
that reached inside you and riveted you. Something so powerful it pierced the heart.

In an instant, the car went streaking past,
out toward the shore. As it sped away, Mrs.
Cary knew she actually felt the mysterious
hush that had fallen over everything before it
lifted.

In a moment, the car was a speck in the
distance. As it vanished, Tony strained to
catch a last glimpse and breathed, "Oh."

Then the car was gone, leaving the three of them trying to understand exactly what had just happened.

Once again it was just another oppressively hot day, with nothing unusual about it beyond the soaring temperature — or so it seemed.

Inside the red convertible, the girl, dressed completely in black, tapped her red fingernails against the wheel in time to a tune she was playing in her head. She pressed her red lips together for a moment and then smiled. It was a perfect, dazzling smile.

Not a single bead of sweat marred the perfection of her skin. It was as if the girl didn't feel the heat, she went *through* it . . . as if she wasn't a part of the atmosphere . . . she was *above* it.

Still smiling, the girl tossed back her black hair and looked out at her surroundings. There were white picket fences in front of many of the yards. All of the houses looked old, but all were well-kept, many newly painted. Quaint was a word that came to mind.

As she drove along, the houses became fewer and fewer. Soon there were only trees on one side of the road, while the other fell away onto a rocky coastline.

The girl drove on, heading out toward the

beach. More particularly, she was headed out toward Sharkey's, a seaside diner that was a teen summer hangout. The girl had never been there before — but she knew exactly where it was.

Inside Sharkey's diner, pandemonium had erupted. In the heat that made even the beach unbearable, kids had come pouring in, shirts sticking damply to chests and backs, tendrils of hair clinging to foreheads and necks.

Lizzie, the teenage waitress, hurried back and forth trying in vain to keep up with the frantic calls and gestures for her attention, looking more harried by the moment.

At a table in a far corner, Jeffrey Thomas squeezed Barbara Matthew's hand. He gently brushed a strand of her long, red-gold hair from her shoulder. "Has it sunk in *yet* that we've really graduated?" he asked, his blue eyes smiling.

Barbara crinkled the turned up nose on her innocent, open face, and shrugged her shoulders. "I don't think I can believe it." She and Jeffrey stared lovingly into each others' eyes.

Across the green Formica table, Miranda Stevens threw up her hands in mock desperation, leaned back in her chair, and stretched out her long coffee-colored legs. "Barbara, when *is* it going to hit you? This is what we've been waiting for. It's like . . ." She looked toward the ceiling, as if hoping to find the right word on its surface. "Now we can get down to some serious business," she said after a moment.

"Business?" echoed her boyfriend Paul Davis. "I move that since we've finally graduated, we concentrate on having some fun!"

"Paul's right," Jeffrey agreed, edging closer to Barbara. "Excuse me," he murmured as he bumped the chair of the girl behind him.

"Oh, that's okay," Vicki Rorsch answered, in a sullen tone. "What's the matter with that waitress?" she complained to her girlfriends at her own table, and anyone else who could hear.

Jeff glanced at the waitress (Lizzie Potter, a girl he knew from school) hurrying back and forth. "Dizzie Lizzie," they called her. Poor Dizzie Lizzie, he thought, watching her.

"Come on Vicki, give it a rest, okay?" Jeffrey sent the words over his shoulder. "She's doing the best she can."

"It's not good enough," Vicki answered. Her silvery lipsticked mouth formed a pout.

Jeffrey didn't pay any attention. He had already turned back to his friends.

Paul started to speak. "Getting back to what we were talking about . . ."

"Which was that we have finally *graduated*. Hurray!" Miranda slapped her hand flat on the table.

"As I was saying before I was interrupted," Paul smiled at Miranda mischievously, "I want to talk about having *fun*." He turned to Jeffrey. "What do you think the odds are of our getting away from Smeal's moving company and sweatshop for a few days?"

Jeffrey chuckled. "Come on, Paul. Haven't we both worked for Mr. Smeal in the summers for the past three years? Don't you know as well as I do that he'll *never* agree to giving us any time off?"

A few moments later, Jeffrey suddenly stopped speaking. He had the peculiar feeling that he'd been talking for a while, but nobody was listening. A hush had rippled through the room like a wave. He noticed how quiet it had become. There was complete silence.

It was *eerie*.

Jeffrey looked at Barbara. Her eyes were wide with wonder, her pupils large and glistening.

Jeffrey glanced at the other side of the table. Paul and Miranda were looking at the same thing Barbara was. Something had happened, and he was the only one who didn't know what it was. He turned to follow their gaze . . . and saw *her*.

On the other side of the diner was a girl more than beautiful. She was breathtaking. She was wearing a tight black tank top and black Lycra pants that clung to her long legs. Her black hair hung to her waist. Her hands, with perfectly manicured red nails, were clasped on the table in front of her.

In the midst of the crowded restaurant, the girl in black sat alone. Being alone amidst a crowd of strangers didn't faze her at all. The girl was calm and completely composed.

Jeffrey watched as Lizzie slowly went past other customers who had, moments ago, been frantically waving her over. She walked straight to the girl in black, her eyes glued to the girl.

After scribbling something on her pad, Lizzie went past tables full of customers again, and walked behind the counter. She came back and set a tall, frosty glass of iced coffee in front of the girl, who smiled slightly and nodded.

As Jeffrey watched, the girl took a sip of the iced coffee, barely touching the glass to her lips before putting it down in front of her again.

Evidently she wasn't hungry, and she wasn't very thirsty. She didn't know anyone in the place. What, then, had she come here for? he wondered.

The girl looked straight ahead. Or was she looking straight at him? Jeffrey could see that she wasn't the slightest bit concerned over the effect she had had on the restaurant.

Here and there, people at the tables began to whisper. Soon there was a buzz of conversation.

"Hey! Hey! What's with you?" Jeffrey heard Vicki calling behind him. From the corner of his eye, he could see her waving her arm at Lizzie, her face contorted in an angry scowl. "Hey, c'mon!" Vicki called again.

Lizzie blinked several times — as if she had suddenly snapped out of a trance. Her harried self again, she walked quickly over to Vicki's table. She opened her mouth to say something, but Vicki stopped her before she could get the words out.

"Take our order! I'd like a small house salad — be sure to put the dressing *on the side*. And I'd like a double chocolate ice-cream soda."

Before Lizzie could hurry away, Vicki put a

restraining hand on her arm. "Wait a minute. Why did you take *her* order before ours, when we've been waiting forever?"

The waitress stood still. Confusion clouded her features. She shook her head. When she spoke, she sounded truly bewildered.

"I don't know. I just couldn't help myself."

Chapter 2

Everyone in the diner sensed that a change had taken place in the room. The atmosphere was strangely electrified. All heads kept turning toward the girl who blazed with an inner light.

The young women in the room were stunned with admiration. The young men ached with longing.

When the waitress brought menus to the table, Barbara accepted hers without taking her eyes from the girl in black. "Who do you suppose that girl *is*?" she breathed into Jeffrey's ear.

Jeffrey looked back at her, seeing the wonder in her eyes. "I don't know," he said. "I've never seen her before." He turned to Paul and Miranda. "Does anybody know who she is?"

"Not me," Paul said, shaking his head. "But

I'll tell you one thing. She's someone who's created quite an impression. Everybody in the place noticed her just like that," he snapped his fingers. "It's kind of strange."

"Maybe she's an actress, or a model," Barbara said. "What do you think, Jeffrey?"

"I think I'm hungry," Jeffrey said, studying his menu.

"Well, I hear *that*," Miranda said, opening her own menu. "I'm more interested in getting some food and something cold to drink than talking about that girl over there. Hey, Jeffrey, maybe we can eat while everybody else is in a state of hypnosis."

"Sounds good to me," Jeffrey replied.

On the other side of the diner, the girl in black sat still as a statue. Occasionally, she turned her head slightly to let her gaze wander and rest briefly on this table or that.

She was aware that she was the topic of conversation at every table. The girl did not relish being the center of attention, but she did not dislike it, either. She didn't bask in the approval of the young people around her, nor was she intimidated by it. She simply acknowledged it as a fact and nothing more.

They all seem so *young*, she thought, as she looked around the room watching the boisterous gestures, hearing the laughter, here and there a voice raised above the others.

The girl turned her attention to the table where Jeffrey and his friends sat. She measured Jeffrey with an appraising stare, taking in the strong, cleanly chiseled features, the brown hair that hung thick and straight below his collar, the way the muscles of his broad shoulders strained against the fabric of his shirt, his clear blue eyes.

In a moment's observation, she understood that the young man was the solid center of his group. She could see it in the way the others directed most of their comments to him, and in the questioning way they often looked at him. Every move he made was strong, deliberate. There was no wasted motion. Here was a boy who sought his own answers, she decided. He never followed the crowd.

She could tell that he was very much in love with the delicate redheaded girl who sat next to him. They had been in love for a long time, from their easy familiarity with each other. As her eyes lingered on Barbara, she sensed openness, sweetness, and honesty — a person who would believe the best of people and usually got it, too, because she was sincere herself.

Just then, her attention was diverted away from watching Barbara by the emphatic motions of a girl at the next table. She stared at Vicki intently, seeing the aggressive thrust of her chin, the almost continuous movement of her lips.

Vicki looked at her, and the girl in black could feel her dislike, the childish resentment because of all the attention being lavished on someone other than herself. The girl in black acknowledged Vicki's dislike with no more emotion than she felt for the approval from the others in the room. It was just another fact.

"I don't see what everyone thinks is so great about her," Jeffrey overheard Vicki saying, her voice edged with an acid whine. He suppressed a grin at how transparently her tone revealed her envy.

"Oh, come on," Vicki's girlfriend Charlene objected. "Look at that outfit — it's incredible. I bet that tank top came from Paris. And look at that *face*. She must spend a fortune on makeup. Because she looks as if she's not wearing any at all!"

Vicki snickered derisively. "Come on, Charlene. I didn't know you were so easily impressed." She swallowed a gulp of ice-cream soda and stabbed viciously at a lettuce leaf.

"Surely you don't think that lipstick she's wearing can compare with the stuff I brought from New York this spring?"

"Well, uh . . ." Charlene began uncertainly.

"Of course it doesn't," Vicki snapped. She paused to chew another lettuce leaf. "And look at that choker she's wearing around her neck. See that red jewel on it? Anyone can tell that stone's a fake."

Vicki shook her head, stabbed another lettuce leaf, chewed, and talked at the same time. Next to her, Charlene watched, fascinated, as Vicki's motions became more and more vigorous. She was *attacking* the lettuce.

"I mean the kind of choker she's wearing is so out-of-date. And it's obviously not an antique — just a cheap imitation."

"But, how can you tell it's not an antique, Vicki?" Charlene protested. "After all — she's clear on the other side of the room."

Vicki stabbed at a remaining piece of lettuce — missed it, stabbed again, and fairly gnashed her teeth into it once or twice before swallowing. When she spoke, she spit out her words.

"Well, I can see it just fine, even if you can't. Honestly, you guys, you can tell a lot about a person from the kind of jewelry they wear and, frankly, that's *tacky*."

As she said the last words, Vicki looked across the room at the girl in black. For a moment, she felt her heart lurch. The girl's glance had rested on her just as she had spoken.

Vicki thought she saw the girl's eyes flicker — as if she'd heard what she said.

Vicki's face grew hot as blood flamed into it. In a single glance, the girl had looked right inside her. She *knew*.

But the panicked sense of shame lasted for only a moment. How could I be so silly? Vicki asked herself. There's no way she could've heard that remark. She's too far away.

Vicki's composure returned. She looked up and saw that her girlfriends were staring at the girl in black again, and talking excitedly. Well, let them stare at her if they didn't know any better. At least they hadn't noticed her brief moment of embarrassment.

Vicki took another sip of her soda, and felt it catch in her throat. Something terrible was happening. She began to gag silently.

Helplessly, Vicki put her hands to her throat. She couldn't think. A white-hot flash of terror had blotted out everything but fear.

She couldn't breathe. Her face turned redder and redder, but she couldn't make a sound.

Vicki was choking — but no one noticed. Her friends weren't paying any attention. Like everyone else, they were watching the girl in black.

Silently, Vicki slipped off her chair to the floor.

Chapter 3

A week had passed since the appearance of the extraordinary girl in black. The oppressive heat had continued, unrelenting. Yet, in spite of the heat that ruled the day, each night the temperature dropped and a smoky fog rolled in. No one had ever seen weather like it in Winthrop. They thought it was unnatural.

Jeffrey, Barbara, and Paul were slumped against the seat of Miranda's blue Camaro as she drove them back from Sharkey's. "I can't believe this is the second weekend in a row we've started for the beach and ended up hanging out at Sharkey's because it's too hot." Paul sighed wearily.

"And every time I go in there, I think about what happened to Vicki, and how really, really strange it was," Miranda spoke up. "I mean, Vicki was choking and nobody even noticed until she fainted."

"Thank goodness she was all right," Barbara said, lifting the mass of red-gold curls off her neck. "I wonder if we'll ever see that amazing girl again. The one who came in dressed in black.

"I've never seen anyone so incredibly gorgeous," Barbara went on. "She looked so *cool*, after coming out of the heat. She had such presence."

"Not again!" Jeffrey groaned. Then he smiled good-naturedly. "Barbara, that's about the millionth time you've mentioned that girl. I don't see what you find so incredible." He lifted a finger and traced the curve of Barbara's cheek. "So she was pretty. But not nearly as pretty as you. Anyway — you might as well forget her since we'll probably never see her again."

"Well, I wonder," said Miranda. She stopped the car in front of Jeffrey's house. "Here we are."

"Hey, thanks for the lift." Jeffrey gave Barbara a quick kiss and opened the door. "You're coming to dinner at about seven, right Barbara?" Jeffrey asked as he stepped out of the car.

"Right." Barbara touched his hand as he left. "I'm bringing your mother a cheesecake for dessert. See you then."

"Bye." Jeffrey stood on the sidewalk and waved as Miranda drove away. Then he started up the walkway that cut through the long front yard. As he walked, his eyes searched the big yard, looking for his six-year-old brother, Tony.

"To-nee! I know you're hiding — come on out or I'm gonna getcha!" Smiling broadly, Jeffrey waited expectantly for his brother to run out from behind a tree. He often hid as soon as he saw Jeffrey arrive — then ran out and "surprised" him. Jeffrey was prepared to register a shocked reaction as soon as his brother snuck up on him.

He waited.

"Tony! Are you out there?"

After a few more moments, Jeffrey turned and started up the walkway again. Funny, he thought — Tony was almost always in the yard playing at this time, no matter how hot it was.

Inside the house, there was silence except for the sound of the pendulum of the grandfather's clock as it swung back and forth.

Where did everybody go? he wondered.

Suddenly realizing how grimy he felt, Jeffrey headed toward the bathroom, when he heard the sound of Tony's laughter coming from the kitchen.

"Hey, Tony? How come you're not playing outside?" he called, striding quickly across the flowered carpet of the living room. As he neared the kitchen he could smell the aroma of cookies.

His brother was sitting on a straight-backed chair at the kitchen table. His mother, wearing jeans and one of his father's old shirts, was taking a batch of cookies from the oven.

Jeffrey touseled his brother's thick brown hair, then lifted him in his muscular arms. "Baking cookies in the afternoon instead of painting, Mom? What's gotten into you?" he asked as he swung Tony high in the air, making him squeal with delight.

"Well, you see, Jeffrey . . ." his mother began.

"No! No!" Tony shrieked. "Let me tell. Let me tell."

"Okay." Jeffrey put his brother down. "You tell me the big news that's making Mom stop working on a picture and bake cookies in the afternoon."

Jeffrey sat down and waited.

"There!" Tony said, pointing over Jeffrey's shoulder.

"There! Behind you!"

Jeffrey turned, and stared at the girl who

had just walked into the room. He recognized her at once. The long black hair, red nails, glowing, translucent skin. It was the girl from the restaurant.

"Hello," she said. "I'm Rebecca Webster."

Chapter 4

Without taking his eyes from the girl, Jeffrey got to his feet and extended his hand to her. She grasped it briefly. Her hand was smooth and cool.

"I saw you out at Sharkey's last week," Jeffrey said.

The girl stared back at him, and Jeffrey noticed how remarkable her eyes were — a deep, smoky violet color he had never seen before. The black lashes were so long they cast shadows on the ivory curve of her cheeks.

"Sharkey's? The place out by the shore?" The girl's voice was a silvery bell. Without waiting for an answer, she inclined her head slightly in a nod. "Yes, I was there."

Jeffrey waited for her to say more. When she didn't, he said, "I'm surprised to see you *here*." He looked questioningly at his mother.

"I'll tell! I'll tell!" Tony said insistently. "Rebecca saved me from the tree! I was scared to come down. And she saved me."

Jeffrey looked from Tony to his mother to Rebecca — and back to Tony. "What? Since when do you get scared climbing trees? You're the tree-climbing champ!"

"This time, I climbed too far. I kept climbing and climbing, and then I was too far up. It was too high," Tony said solemnly. "I wanted to get the kitten," he added.

Mrs. Thomas turned around. "Tony, we've been all over this. There *was* no kitten," she said firmly.

"Yes, there *was*," Tony said, his voice quavering. "It was black, and it had *bright red* eyes. *Special* eyes."

"Tony," his mother said, exasperated. "There was no red-eyed kitten! If there *was*, it would still be in the tree! We couldn't find any kitten."

Tony's lip began to quiver. "There *was* a kitten. I *saw* it. I was going to get it. There *was* a kitten, there *was*." Tony's eyes were starting to fill with tears.

"I know what," Rebecca said, crossing over to Tony. As she bent down to look into his eyes, her hair fell to one side like a black velvet curtain. "I'll bet that it was a pretend kitten, and it *vanished*. Pouf!" She made a graceful gesture in the air.

Tony smiled suddenly. "That's right," he said, looking at Rebecca and beaming.

Jeffrey's mother said incredulously, "You're certainly on his wavelength!" She smiled and shook her head.

"Rebecca was a godsend," she said to Jeffrey. "Tony was calling and I didn't hear a thing. He was getting hysterical, and Rebecca happened to be passing by."

"She climbed the tree and got me down," Tony said with admiration.

Jeffrey regarded Rebecca, trying to imagine the beautiful girl climbing the tree in his front yard.

"It was nothing, really," Rebecca said. A tapered hand flicked a lock of hair over her shoulder. Her crimson fingernails sparkled.

"Well — I'm certainly glad you were there, Rebecca," Jeffrey's mother said heartily. She glanced at the clock on the wall. "Shoot! Barbara's coming to dinner and I'm making bouillabaisse. It'll take forever. I've got to get started." She opened a cabinet and began pulling out pans.

"Well, it was good to meet you, Tony. Thanks for the hospitality, Mrs. Thomas. Nice to meet you, Jeffrey." Rebecca looked into his eyes and flashed a radiant smile.

"Oh. Well, thanks, Rebecca!" Mrs. Thomas said as they all walked Rebecca to the door. "Do stop by again. I wish you'd take some cookies with you, since you didn't have any. If you wait just a minute, I'll wrap up some for you."

Rebecca shook her head, making her hair ripple around her shoulders like a wave.

"Wait a minute!" Mrs. Thomas said suddenly as Rebecca started to leave. "I have a wonderful idea! Why don't you stay for dinner? There will be plenty, and you can meet Jeffrey's girlfriend, Barbara. What do you say?"

Rebecca silently considered the invitation. She fingered the black choker with the ruby stone. "Why, thank you, Mrs. Thomas," she said after a moment. "That's so kind of you. I'm sure dinner would be wonderful, but I wouldn't dream of imposing."

"You wouldn't be imposing," Mrs. Thomas began, but suddenly fell silent. "Oh, my gosh," she gasped, looking out the picture window in the living room. "Will you look at that!"

Jeffrey turned toward the window and drew his breath in sharply. When he'd come into the house, the sun had been blazing — the sky blue and cloudless.

Now it was an ominous steely gray that held the promise of something dangerous to come.

As Jeffrey stared out the window, the sky got even darker until it was pitch-black. A low rumble of thunder shook the air, followed by a whip-crack of lightning.

Then the sky opened up and a downpour descended.

Chapter 5

Outside, chaos had erupted. The floodgates of the sky burst open, and torrents of rain poured out.

A shroud of smoke-colored fog had descended and hovered over the horizon. Through its darkness, brilliant snakes of lightning cracked and exploded.

Thunderous rumblings shook the air, adding to the turmoil of light and sound. The storm lashed the landscape, whipping it into a frenzy. The leaves on the trees rustled as if raising their voices in protest.

Jeffrey's mother backed away from the window, her face pale, drawn, and tight. Jeffrey stared at the overwhelming spectacle, awestruck at the sudden surge of force.

In the midst of gazing at the storm, Jeffrey caught sight of Rebecca from the corner of an eye, and turned to look at her. He was caught up in what he saw.

Rebecca stood close to the window and showed not the slightest trace of fear. Instead, her face was electrified with excitement.

"Rebecca . . ."

Rebecca turned and gazed at Jeffrey, her entire being ablaze with emotion. A bolt of lightning flashed across the sky and was reflected in her eyes. She looked as if possessed by the storm. When she spoke it was with the voice of someone in a trance.

"It's beautiful, isn't it? Wild, with a life of its own. You can feel it, can't you?"

Rebecca looked deep into Jeffrey's eyes and he found himself captured, unable to look away. He gazed back at her and he, too, was caught up in the fury and majesty of the storm. He could see it, feel it, through her eyes.

"Boom! Boom! Boom!" Tony cried joyfully as another thunderbolt crashed. For Jeffrey, the spell was broken.

There was something about Rebecca's eyes, Jeffrey thought as he looked away from her. They were hypnotic — but there was something else. He had looked into her eyes and felt as if there was something there he couldn't see. Something hidden and powerful.

"Well, Mother Nature seems very angry with us," Mrs. Thomas said with forced lightness in her voice. She turned to Rebecca, who was standing quite calm and very still.

"Rebecca, there's one thing about the storm we can be thankful for." Mrs. Thomas pushed strands of pale brown hair from her forehead with light, quick gestures. "Now you'll simply have to stay for dinner."

Rebecca tilted her head a little to one side. Then a smile lit up her face.

"Thanks so much. I'd like that. And, Mrs. Thomas, I'd love to help with the bouillabaisse."

"But I thought we could play a game," Tony said eagerly, his eyes fixed on Rebecca's face.

"Who says we can't?" Rebecca asked in her lilting voice as she looked down at the boy. "Come along," she motioned for him to walk beside her. "We'll play a game while we help your mother cook."

"Rebecca's my new friend," Tony said proudly. He looped his thumbs through the straps of his overalls and strutted as he followed her into the kitchen.

She's certainly won Tony over, Jeffrey thought as he watched them go into the kitchen. He wondered just how surprised Barbara would be when she saw Rebecca.

In fact, Barbara's reaction was stronger than Jeffrey had imagined. When she first saw Rebecca, she seemed too stunned to speak. During dinner, she hung on Rebecca's every word as the girl entertained them all with stories of her amazing life.

"My parents go all over the world looking for art, antiques, and so forth, which they acquire for museums and private collectors. When I was a child, they usually took me with them. We went to Italy and France several times, but lots of other places, too. I especially liked it when we went away from the big cities and took little trips into the country."

"That's so interesting," said Barbara, leaning forward. "I've hardly been out of Winthrop. Well, except for a trip to Florida with my parents. Oh — and those bicycle trips Jeffrey and I have been taking in the fall for the past few years." She and Jeffrey exchanged warm glances.

Just then the door opened and Mr. Thomas entered. He took off his jacket with the Thomas Hardware store emblem on the back and hung it on the coat tree. Then he crossed to the table. "I'm so glad you're home." Mrs. Thomas rose and kissed him on the cheek. "Even though the store isn't far away, I couldn't help being worried about the storm."

"It wasn't as bad as it looked — but it's got things in a big mess," Mr. Thomas said with a dismissive wave of his hand. "The roads are all muddy. Getting anywhere takes forever."

His eyes rested on Rebecca. "I see we have a guest."

Rebecca was introduced and Mr. Thomas sat down at the table, helping himself to a ladleful of the fish stew.

"Would you like some more bouillabaisse, Rebecca?" Mrs. Thomas asked. She looked at Rebecca's bowl and drew back, startled. "Why — is something wrong? You haven't touched a thing."

"Oh." Rebecca glanced down at her plate as if noticing it for the first time. She rested a tapered, ivory hand at the base of her slender throat, performing the casual gesture with infinite grace. "I'm sorry. I was enjoying the company so much I'm afraid I haven't given food a thought," she said in her silvery voice. "Not to mention all the excitement of moving into a new house. I hope you'll forgive me."

"Well, of course. Don't give it another thought," Mrs. Thomas insisted.

"Sounds perfectly understandable," Jeffrey's father said, peering at Rebecca over his glasses. "It just means more for me." He took another ladleful of stew. "Tell us about your new home."

"All right." Absently, Rebecca gave her plate a little shove. "It's funny how it happened. My parents always wanted to find a house on the seashore. Not just any house. *The* house." Rebecca looked around the table.

"It seemed as if we'd been looking *forever*. And then" — she snapped her fingers — "just like that, we stumbled on the place by accident."

"What place?" Jeffrey prompted.

"It's out by the bluffs, overlooking the sea. There's a wonderful view. I love looking at the sea."

"My goodness!" Mrs. Thomas exclaimed. "You must mean the old Branford place. Why — no one has lived there for ages. It's ancient, and — so isolated."

"I rather like the solitude, actually. I'm fixing the place up while my parents are in Europe on business."

"You're staying there *alone?*" Barbara was wide-eyed.

"Yes." Rebecca answered simply, as if she failed to see anything remarkable about that.

Jeffrey could see that Barbara's admiration for Rebecca had risen even higher than before. Then a thought occurred to him.

"Wait a minute, you didn't drive over here, did you Rebecca?"

Rebecca shook her head.

"Well, the bluffs are miles from here. At least *fifteen* miles away. How is it that you just happened to be passing by our house?"

Rebecca looked away for a moment. When she replied, she gazed steadily into Jeffrey's eyes. "Are the bluffs really that far away? I'd never have thought so. I suppose I got caught up in exploring my new surroundings. I find it so refreshing to be outside, feeling the sun on my face."

"In this heat?" Jeffrey asked quizzically.

"Well, the heat doesn't seem to bother you in the slightest, Rebecca," Barbara spoke up. "You're positively glowing."

Rebecca accepted the compliment with a slightly upward curve of her mouth.

Mrs. Thomas clasped her hands under her chin and looked at Rebecca. "Well, I'm certainly glad you love to walk, and you happened to be passing by. It's been a pleasure meeting you — not to mention the way you helped Tony out of the tree. I think everything worked out perfectly."

"Yes," Rebecca answered with a faraway look in her eyes, her expression thoughtful. "Everything worked out just perfectly."

Chapter 6

"Thank you for driving me home, Jeffrey," Rebecca's voice was as clear as crystal. The glare of the roadside lights lit up her face. Such harsh light did not flatter most people. But it caressed Rebecca's delicate features, illuminating them so that she was as breathtaking to look at as if her face were bathed in candlelight.

"No problem," Jeffrey replied, never taking his eyes from the road. He sat perfectly straight, clasping the steering wheel with both hands.

They drove on in silence toward the outskirts of town. From there they headed onto the road that led out to the cliffs, where Rebecca's house was located. Every so often, Jeffrey flicked on the wipers to remove the fine layer of mist that settled on the windshield.

"What do you want to do with your life, Jeffrey?" Rebecca asked, suddenly looking directly at him.

"Study law," Jeffrey replied without hesitation. "Eventually, I hope to become a judge."

At the sound of his words, Rebecca recoiled as if a whip had lashed at her body. She stiffened, and a shadow darkened her eyes. Her hands were clenched into fists in her lap, the red nails pressing into her palms. When she spoke, her voice was icy cold.

"Why do you want to do that? So you can accuse people of committing crimes, and sentence them to death?"

Stunned by her angry tone and the bitterness in her voice, Jeffrey looked at her sharply. He saw that her mouth was set in a grim, hard line.

"I can't imagine why you'd jump to such a conclusion," he said, with surprise, returning his gaze to the road. He noticed the way that the mist had draped itself over the boulders at the roadside, making them look like gravestones.

"The reason I'm going to practice law is to *help* people, to work for equal rights and fair treatment. Too many people don't believe in justice anymore."

Rebecca didn't reply. "Turn here," she said after a moment, indicating a road to the left. Her voice still had its icy edge.

Jeffrey turned down the narrow road. It was flanked by trees on either side. They grew closely together, and their branches, thick with leaves, formed a canopy overhead that blocked out the light of the moon.

After the car had bounced along the dirt road for what seemed like an eternity, they came to an iron gate. "Here it is," Rebecca said.

Jeffrey stopped the car. Rebecca's house lay beyond the gate, at the end of a path. Jeffrey looked at the house in amazement.

It was hard to imagine a person living alone in so desolate a place. In the glow of the headlights Jeffrey saw a decrepit, weathered structure. It was in such an advanced state of disrepair it actually looked decayed.

Cavernous windows gaped like huge hollow eyes. Some had rough wooden planks nailed over them.

Not just any house, *the* house. Jeffrey recalled Rebecca's words. The idea that anyone had gone searching for such an eerie dwelling made him shudder.

"Would you like to see the house?" Rebecca asked.

"See the house?" Jeffrey echoed in surprise. He looked at Rebecca and saw her eyes burning with intensity. "I can't."

"What a pity. I had hoped you would want to be friends," Rebecca said in a seductive tone.

"Being friendly has nothing to do with it, Rebecca. If I didn't want to be friendly, I wouldn't have driven you home. It's late, and I promised Barbara I'd call her when I got home. That's all."

"I understand," Rebecca said slowly. "I'll show you the house some other time, then. Sometime soon."

She got out of the car and walked up the path without a backward glance.

By the time Jeffrey returned home, it was quite late. The windows in his house were dark. He was drowsy, his brain clouded with the desire for sleep.

He pulled the car into the garage. As he got out, the noise of his shoes echoed on the concrete. He clicked on the light, and frowned at the bulb's loud *pop*. He was plunged into darkness.

Light shone dimly through the glass panes of the door that led from the garage to the kitchen. Guided by the light, Jeffrey made his way toward the door, and reached for the doorknob.

Suddenly, he froze. Someone — or *something* was watching him. He hadn't heard a noise, but he felt a presence.

Jeffrey's eyes searched the shadows for something lurking there. His heart pounded.

Then, out of the darkness he saw two burning red eyes. As he stared, he could make out a form crouched in a corner. The red-eyed kitten, he thought. Tony had seen it after all.

The thing in the corner suddenly darted across the floor in a slithering motion. Jeffrey caught the movement of a whiplike tail.

It was not a kitten, that much he knew. What was it? A rat? he thought with revulsion.

Jeffrey heard a scraping sound and whirled around. Again, he saw the burning red eyes. The thing hissed at him.

As Jeffrey watched in astonishment, the thing leaped to the top of the car and hissed again. The hiss turned into an angry snarl.

Jeffrey was filled with nausea as he gazed at the creature. Neither a cat, nor a rat, it looked like something not of this world.

It was hideous. Almost reptilian. It looked back at him with an evil grin that showed a row of razor-sharp teeth. As it walked toward him, he could hear its claws clicking against the metal surface of the car.

The thing's tail jerked angrily back and forth. Its red eyes bore into Jeffrey's.

It gave another menacing snarl, and launched itself into the air, straight for Jeffrey's face.

Jeffrey leaped backward, instinctively raising his arms to shield his eyes. He braced himself for the searing pain of claws slashing his skin. In an instant, the thing loomed before him, so close he could smell its reeking breath.

And then it vanished into the air.

Chapter 7

Barbara squinted and lifted a hand to shield her eyes from the glare of the sun. Such a strange-looking sky, she thought. Overcast, yet the sun shone through, lighting up the day with an eerie sort of brilliance. The air was thick with humidity.

Barbara stood at the entrance to the brand new Seaside Mall, halfway between Winthrop and the next town. She scanned the parking lot for a glimpse of Rebecca.

Last night, when they'd met at the Thomases', Barbara had suggested showing Rebecca the new mall. She'd offered to give Rebecca a ride, but Rebecca had insisted in following along in her own car.

It would have been fun to chat as they drove along. Barbara shrugged. Oh, well, there would be plenty of time to get to know each

41

other while they shopped. Then they'd meet the gang at Sharkey's.

Where in the world was Rebecca?

Barbara sighed. As she waited, her thoughts turned to Jeffrey. Last night was the first time he hadn't called her when he'd said he would. It was so unlike him.

He'd called this morning, though. He told her he'd fallen dead asleep as soon as he'd gotten home. Then he said he'd had a strange nightmare. In the dream, he was attacked by a hideous creature like nothing he'd ever seen. It had disappeared suddenly, just as he thought it was about to slash his face. In all the years that Barbara had known Jeffrey, he'd never mentioned having a nightmare before.

Then Barbara saw Rebecca. She waved, and Rebecca came toward her, moving so gracefully that she appeared to be floating along.

Rebecca's hair was pulled back from her face and caught at the nape of her neck. It hung streaming down her back, swaying as she walked.

She wore a high-necked, black sleeveless shirt made of fabric that shimmered in the sun. Her black jeans clung to the curves of her long, slender legs.

As Rebecca approached, Barbara saw that she looked fresh and cool and marvelously alive despite the unrelenting heat. In seconds, the girl in black was beside her.

Barbara lifted her heavy mass of red curls from her damp neck and let them fall. "Rebecca, you look so lovely and cool. I should have worn my hair up. It feels like I'm wearing a wool hat."

"But your hair looks beautiful." Rebecca spun around in a graceful, fluid motion. "The mall must be air-conditioned," she said over her shoulder. "Come on. Let's go inside."

Rebecca was already walking through the doorway. Barbara hurried to keep up as Rebecca headed toward the center of the mall's courtyard, from which walkways to stores stretched in four directions. The courtyard was lit up by a huge fountain and water leaped in plumes, arcs, and swirls, illuminated by colored lights.

"They call it the dancing waters," Barbara told Rebecca, watching her gaze at the water with an expression of fascination. Her complexion glowed and her thick lashes cast shadows along the curves of her cheeks. The light from the fountain formed a halo around her, giving her an aura of mysterious beauty.

"Do you always wear black?" Barbara asked abruptly, the words out of her mouth almost before she realized she'd said them.

For a moment Rebecca said nothing; she just stood gazing into the fountain. Then she turned to Barbara slowly. "I like black," she said, definitely.

Barbara felt suddenly chilled and uncomfortable. She couldn't read Rebecca's expression. Did I say something wrong? she wondered.

And then Rebecca flashed a dazzling smile, and everything was all right again.

"Can you think of an easier way to coordinate outfits than by having everything in black?" She laughed lightly, a warm, inviting sound.

Relieved, Barbara laughed, too. "I never thought of it that way."

All around them, throngs of people were milling about, some dawdling, some hurrying to and fro. Here and there groups of teens could be seen just hanging out. As they passed by, people cast curious, admiring glances at Rebecca.

"What would you like to do first, Rebecca?" Barbara asked. "Look at some jewelry . . . or makeup?" She hoped Rebecca would say "makeup." Barbara wanted to discover what Rebecca used to look so incredibly stunning.

Rebecca was looking around as if she'd never seen a mall before. "I want to go shopping for clothes," she answered firmly.

As they headed toward the shops, the crowd parted before them. People took one look at Rebecca and stepped aside and stared. "She's beautiful," a small girl said, pointing at her.

"You must have had loads of boyfriends where you came from," Barbara remarked.

Rebecca's hair swung as she shook her head. "No. I went out on dates, but there was no one special." She glanced at Barbara from under her lashes. "Certainly not special the way Jeffrey is to you."

Barbara's eyes took on a dreamy quality. "We've been going together practically forever. We were even friends in nursery school."

"Tell me about him," Rebecca prompted. Her eyes never left Barbara's face.

Barbara needed little encouragement. "Jeffrey's different — he's more mature than other boys his age. He has high ideals. And he's very independent.

"Jeffrey has so many talents," Barbara went on. "He paints wonderful pictures. It's something he never talks about."

Barbara stopped talking suddenly. She was afraid that she was going on too much about Jeffrey. But when she glanced at Rebecca, she saw that she was watching her intently, with an expression of rapt attention.

So Barbara stopped wondering if she was talking about Jeffrey too much and allowed herself to go on and on about her favorite subject. She talked endlessly about Jeffrey as she and Rebecca went to shop after shop.

About twenty minutes later, they were in Rags, a boutique that carried the newest styles. Barbara stood in front of a mirror, wearing a pale green minidress that flattered her delicate coloring and the shimmering red hair that flowed in curls over her shoulders.

Jeffrey will love this, she said to herself. "I'm going to take this one," Barbara said enthusiastically to Rebecca.

Rebecca came gliding over. "It looks terrific on you. It makes you look . . . sweet."

Then Barbara saw the reflection of them side by side in the mirror. There was Barbara in the pale green dress with a gathered bodice and tiny yellow dots.

Beside the reflection of Barbara was the reflection of Rebecca, her black tank top and jeans clinging to her, setting off her perfectly curved figure. Her alabaster skin was like satin. She looked elegant, with no jewelry except her black choker.

Suddenly, Barbara didn't like her "look" anymore. The dress that had seemed perfect a moment ago now seemed too young, unsophisticated, and fussy.

"Maybe I won't take this dress after all," Barbara said. "Let's look in some more stores."

"You're right," Rebecca agreed. "You could do better."

Four hours later, Barbara was sure that they had been to every store in the mall. Although Rebecca was the one who had suggested shopping for clothes, she hadn't tried anything on. She'd hardly looked at anything for herself.

Meanwhile, Barbara had tried on dress after dress, growing more and more frustrated. She hadn't bought a thing. Every time she thought she liked something, she would look at Rebecca, or see her reflection in a mirror, and then the dress just wasn't right anymore.

"I've had it." Barbara threw herself down on a bench in front of the dancing waters. "I feel as if I've run a marathon and I've nothing to show for it." She crossed her legs and rubbed an ankle.

"I was hoping to find a new dress to wear on my next date with Jeffrey."

"Don't worry," Rebecca told her. "I'm sure

you'll find something another day. Let's go and meet Jeffrey and your friends." Before Rebecca had gotten the words out, she had already turned toward the door.

"Hold on a minute," Barbara said. She wondered where Rebecca got her energy. When they'd stopped for lunch at the Yogurt Palace, Barbara had had a dish of banana swirl with granola topping — but Rebecca had only ordered a cup of coffee. Yet she looked as vibrant as when they'd arrived at the mall.

As she looked at Rebecca, Barbara suddenly had an idea. She wondered why she hadn't thought of it before.

"Rebecca, you go ahead to Sharkey's. I want to try on something else."

"No, I'll come with you."

"No. I want this to be a kind of surprise. You go ahead and I'll meet you."

"All right then," Rebecca agreed without a moment's hesitation.

Barbara glanced up to say good-bye, and drew her breath in sharply. When Rebecca had spoken to her an instant before, she was standing right beside her.

Now Rebecca was gone.

Chapter 8

Heads turned as Rebecca entered Sharkey's. Many of the people had been there for Rebecca's first appearance. Others had seen her, maybe even spoken to her, around the town. There were looks of recognition. No one who saw Rebecca once ever forgot her. She left a lasting impression.

Vicki, who was sitting at a table with her boyfriend Trent Marliss, remembered Rebecca immediately. Her memories of their first encounter were less than fond.

What happened next did not please her.

"Hey, hey, Rebecca," Trent was calling and waving wildly.

Vicki hadn't had time to get over the shock that *he knew her*, when Rebecca was heading her way.

"Thank you for helping me with my car trouble the other day, Trent," Rebecca said as she stood by the table, shimmering with beauty.

"No problem. Glad to help." Vicki saw Trent flash Rebecca a big grin.

Any minute now, he's going to duck his head and say, "Aw, shucks," Vicki thought with disgust. Even though she'd grown tired of Trent and was merely waiting for the right moment to break up with him, she didn't care for the way he was looking at Rebecca. She, herself, had inspired that same look on the faces of other girls' boyfriends at times, and she knew very well what it meant. It meant that she had overshadowed them.

Vicki cast a sidelong glance at Rebecca. Car trouble — ha! she thought. She didn't believe that one for a minute.

As Trent and Rebecca talked, Vicki tried to appear disinterested and aloof. She pretended to look at who was at the other tables, and she poked at her food. She didn't know how long she could keep it up, but every time Rebecca started to walk away, Trent asked her another question.

Then things went from bad to worse.

"Trent, you haven't introduced me to your friend," Rebecca said in her crystal clear voice.

Vicki cringed. Now she'd have to look at Rebecca. There was no way out. She dreaded seeing the smug satisfaction her own face had so often worn when *she* had eclipsed another girl for a boy's attention.

Vicki reluctantly raised her eyes. But instead of the superior smirk she expected to see, she was surprised by Rebecca's friendliness.

"Hello, Vicki." Rebecca smiled, displaying dazzlingly white teeth. "I've been wanting to meet you. You know, Trent couldn't *stop* talking about you the other day. He was telling me you design all your own clothes. That's quite a talent."

Now it was Trent's turn to be shocked. He couldn't remember giving Vicki a thought when he had been with Rebecca, much less mentioning her name.

Trent realized his surprise was showing and covered it up quickly. If he hadn't told Rebecca about Vicki designing clothes, how would she know? And why would she say he'd talked about Vicki if he hadn't?

I *must* have said something, Trent decided. It was so strange. He had a queasy sensation in the pit of his stomach.

Vicki, meanwhile, had been completely won over. It was an unfamiliar feeling, for Vicki generally didn't care for girls who were too attractive. Yet any trace of malice she felt for Rebecca had vanished completely.

"Sit down for a minute, won't you, Rebecca, so we can talk?"

Several tables away, Jeffrey, Miranda, and Paul were waiting for Barbara and Rebecca. It was Miranda who first noticed that Rebecca had arrived. She watched, fascinated, as Vicki threw back her head and laughed at something Rebecca said.

"Hey, hey, check this out." Miranda cut in on something Paul was saying to Jeffrey. The two boys turned to follow her gaze.

"Have you ever seen Vicki act that way around another girl *that* good-looking?" Miranda asked in a tone of hushed amazement. "I mean, Vicki looks *really* friendly."

"Whoa. Maybe she's just not herself today," Paul said. "Wouldn't it be great if she stayed that way?"

"Well, you know," Jeffrey said evenly, "Vicki's probably not so bad really. Her dad's got a lot of money, and she's been spoiled rotten all her life, that's all. Maybe she's starting to grow up."

Just then, Rebecca rose from the table and started coming their way.

"Hello, Jeffrey," she said, sliding into a seat across from him.

"Hello, Rebecca." Jeffrey introduced her to Paul and Miranda.

"Before you say anything else, Rebecca, we want to know how you got the queen of mean to look so friendly," Paul said.

Rebecca smiled. "I'm good at that."

"It certainly looks that way," Paul nodded. "Want to give us a few pointers?"

As if she had not heard the question, Rebecca turned to Jeffrey. "Barbara tells me you paint, Jeffrey. So do I."

"Barbara's exaggerating," Jeffrey said, his eyes looking past Rebecca, toward the door. "She liked some pictures I painted, but I just play around with it. That's all."

"Oh." Rebecca's voice was almost inaudible. "I'd love to show you some of my paintings," she said, after a moment. She looked into Jeffrey's eyes. "Why don't you come over tonight?"

Miranda raised her eyebrows and looked at Paul.

"Sorry, I can't do it," Jeffrey said immediately. "I'm taking Barbara to the movies. There's a new legal thriller I want to see."

Rebecca's face tightened.

Jeffrey drummed his fingers on the table. "By the way, where is Barbara? Didn't she leave the mall with you?"

"No." Rebecca reached behind and pulled the velvet band from her hair with a graceful gesture. Loosened, it fell in a tangle of waves around her shoulders. "She said she had some more shopping to do. I'm sure she'll be along soon."

"She's here," Miranda said looking toward the door with a stunned expression.

Jeffrey turned and saw Barbara. She was wearing a clinging black skirt and matching top. It was exactly what Rebecca wore. The effect was startling. Barbara was out of place in the clothes. The black outfit drowned her delicate coloring.

As Barbara walked toward the table, Miranda glanced at Rebecca. The girl didn't look the least bit surprised. Miranda thought there was something strangely secretive about the smile that played on her lips.

"What do you think of my new outfit?" Barbara asked, breathlessly, sitting down beside Jeffrey.

"It's different from anything I've ever seen you wear," Jeffrey said vaguely.

Barbara waited, looking at him expectantly.

"Barbara, you look wonderful," Rebecca spoke up. The conviction in her voice was absolute. "You look terribly sophisticated." Rebecca gazed steadily at Barbara.

"You think so? I'm so glad!" Barbara bubbled enthusiastically. "That's just the look I was aiming for."

Jeffrey ran a hand gently over Barbara's hair. "Let's get something to eat, then we can take a drive before we head over to the movie."

"Great, I'm *starving*." Barbara looked over at Rebecca. "You must be hungry, too, Rebecca. You didn't eat a thing all day."

"No." Rebecca's eyes flickered impatiently. "Nothing for me."

"Goodness." Barbara's eyes widened. "You never eat!" She folded her menu. "I'm going to get a cheeseburger and french fries."

Soon the waitress came over and took everyone's order. Rebecca asked for an iced coffee.

As the others talked, Miranda studied Rebecca. Quite a presence, she said to herself. She's certainly beautiful. Such amazing eyes . . . so intense.

Miranda noticed that regardless of who Rebecca spoke to, she had kept her eyes riveted on Barbara since Barbara had arrived. There was something unsettling about it.

By and by, Miranda noticed something else. Barbara was growing quieter and quieter. She seemed distracted. After a while she slumped listlessly in her seat.

By the time the waitress brought their order, Barbara was quite pale. Her face had taken on a greenish hue.

"I don't feel well," Barbara said, eyeing the food the waitress had just put in front of her.

"What's the matter?" Jeffrey's voice was full of concern.

Barbara hunched her shoulders. "I'm sick to my stomach. It's awful." She took a deep breath. "I guess I did too much running around today."

Jeffrey got to his feet. "I'll take you home."

Barbara shook her head. "No, Jeffrey. You stay here. I'd rather go home by myself. Call me later, okay?"

Before Jeffrey could say anything, Barbara got up and walked quickly to the door. Too startled to move, Jeffrey watched her leave. After Barbara had gone, no one said a word.

After a few moments, Rebecca broke the silence. "Well, now you can come over after all, Jeffrey," she said in honeyed tones. "I'll expect you around eight o'clock."

Chapter 9

Steely gray clouds shrouded the sky, making it unnaturally dark for a summer evening. The temperature had begun to drop. Already, the mists were rolling in, with the promise of heavy fog to come.

Driving along toward Rebecca's house, Jeffrey was forced to turn on the headlights to see the road. He glanced at his watch. Seven forty-five. It was unusual to need lights this early.

He reached up to adjust the rearview mirror and was startled as he saw his own reflection. Shadows fell sharply across his face, making his features look stony and his eyes appear sunken deep in their sockets. He took a deep breath and turned onto the side road that led to Rebecca's house.

What am I doing? Jeffrey asked himself

again, as he had several times along the way. *What made me come out here?*

He wasn't interested in looking at Rebecca's paintings. When she had asked him, the invitation had struck Jeffrey as odd. It had made him want to avoid her.

And yet here I am. Jeffrey reached the iron gate that stood in front of Rebecca's house. He turned off the engine and got out of the car.

"Incredible," he breathed, as he gazed at the house. Once again he was struck by the air of desolation about the place. In the darkness that hovered at the edge of night, the house looked even lonelier and more decayed than the first time he'd seen it. Mist draped around the structure like huge clinging cobwebs.

Jeffrey was aware of the silence that hung in the air. There was no chirping of crickets, no whispering of leaves on the trees.

Leaves on the trees, Jeffrey echoed in his mind. He tilted his head back and looked around. There were no leaves on the trees in the yard. There were only bare branches.

Looking carefully at the ground, he noticed that there was no grass, either. There was only dry earth, here and there a patch of dry weeds.

A hollow feeling twisted into Jeffrey's stomach. A prickling sensation tightened the muscles at the back of his neck.

The whole place was overcome with blight.

Suddenly, Jeffrey wanted to turn around and go home. And yet, after he'd put his hand on the door handle and started to open the car door, he changed his mind and decided to stay.

Jeffrey's shoes made a hard, gritty sound as he crossed the dirt yard. He walked up the steps onto the porch and knocked on the door.

When there was no answer, he peered into one of the cavernous windows. What he saw made Jeffrey take a single, startled step back.

There was no furniture. No sign of life at all.

The house was empty.

And then a shadow stepped toward him and said his name.

"Jeffrey."

The shadow had eyes that burned with intensity. It was Rebecca, Jeffrey realized as he continued to stare. Her face was hidden by the hood of her black cloak.

"It's so quiet, I thought perhaps you weren't here," Jeffrey said.

Rebecca threw back her hood. Her alabaster skin gleamed in the moonlight that filtered through the clouds. "Let's go inside."

Rebecca opened the door. It groaned as it moved on rusted hinges.

Jeffrey followed Rebecca into the house. Their footsteps echoed in the emptiness.

They entered a room lit up by dozens of candles.

"There's a problem with the electricity," Rebecca said. "But this is really rather beautiful."

She took off her cloak, the movement like music. When she turned to Jeffrey, the sight of her took his breath away.

In the candlelight, Rebecca shimmered. Her hair fell about her shoulders in gossamer strands. Her violet eyes, surrounded by thick lashes, blazed with fragments of light.

She was so beautiful. Jeffrey felt that he had looked at Rebecca many times, but he had never really seen her. This was the first time.

Rebecca stood still and let him look at her. They gazed at each other in silence.

Miles away, Barbara sat on her bed and stared at the telephone. She had just called Jeffrey's house. His mother had told her that Jeffrey'd gone out. He hadn't said where he was going, or when he'd be back.

Barbara rested her chin in her hands. Oh,

well, she thought. She'd hear from him. Jeffrey called her every night.

Barbara got up off the bed and walked to her dressing table. She hoped Jeffrey would call soon. She didn't feel the least bit sick anymore, and she wanted to go out.

Sitting down on the chair in front of the dressing table, Barbara looked in the mirror above it. Tonight she wanted to wear the new black tank top and black pants she'd bought today. The outfit was so sophisticated — like something Rebecca would wear. If only she could do something with her hair.

Looking in the mirror, Barbara pulled up her mass of red-gold curls. Holding them off her neck, she turned her head this way and that. There must be something I can do with this hair, she thought. But what?

Barbara sighed. It was almost nine o'clock. She stared at the telephone again, willing it to ring.

"Why don't I show you a painting," Rebecca said, still staring steadily into Jeffrey's eyes.

Jeffrey swallowed hard. "All right."

Rebecca gestured toward a corner of the room. For the first time, Jeffrey saw an easel there, with a painting on it. He walked over to it. "It's a picture of a graveyard," he said in a hushed voice.

"Yes," Rebecca said softly. "There's one near here." She came and stood next to him, so close that her silken hair almost touched his face.

Jeffrey stared at the painting. It was remarkable, really, he thought. It looked so real.

As he stared, Jeffrey felt the picture pulling him, beckoning him. It was as if he was being swept into the painting. He was standing in the graveyard at night. Mist swirled around the headstones.

So vivid.

Jeffrey's heart began to pound. Something disturbing was happening to him. He put a hand to his temples.

Blood was rushing through his head. He heard it roaring in his ears. He felt dizzy.

Wrenching his eyes from the painting, Jeffrey took in a great gulp of air. The room was spinning. Rebecca was looking at him strangely, her eyes glittering in the candlelight.

"I've got to go," Jeffrey said. "I'm feeling sick." Without another word, he turned and left.

Jeffrey's hands were shaking so that it was hard to insert the key in the ignition. Somehow, he got the car started. His mind was a blank as he headed onto the main road.

After he had been traveling for a few minutes, however, he began to recover. What came over me? he wondered. He hoped he wasn't coming down with something. He had to work for Mr. Smeal the next day on a moving job.

By the time Jeffrey reached his house, he felt fine. But he slept fitfully, tossing and turning all night. He had nightmares in which he walked in a graveyard where red-eyed monsters lurked behind the gravestones, waiting to pounce. Each time he saw one, it flew at him, with pointed fangs bared, and razor-sharp talons poised to strike. And then it vanished into the air.

Chapter 10

The following morning Jeffrey overslept. He jerked awake, automatically turning toward the electric clock on his night table. When he saw that it was after nine, his heart skipped a beat. He must have forgotten to set the alarm.

Now he would be at least an hour late by the time he got to the address where he was to meet Paul and Mr. Smeal. Mr. Smeal was cranky even when things ran smoothly. Now he was going to have a fit.

Jeffrey's eyelids felt leaden. Oh, no, he groaned inwardly as he hauled himself up. For a moment he sat on the edge of the bed, feeling groggy. He ran a hand through his hair. He couldn't remember ever having overslept when he had to work.

With an effort, Jeffrey pulled himself out of bed and walked slowly to the closet, dragging himself along. His arms and legs felt heavy, as if they had weights on them. His movements were sluggish and clumsy.

Everything was a struggle. He kept telling himself to get going. But in spite of the urgency he felt, he just couldn't get moving.

As he dressed, his mind drifted back to the previous night. Memories flooded into his brain.

In his mind's eye, Jeffrey saw Rebecca, her beauty burning brighter than the candlelight on her face. Her eyes looked into his own so deeply he felt that she could see inside his soul. The memory was so strong that for a fleeting instant Rebecca was there in the room, her radiant presence beside him.

Then Jeffrey began to feel the same dizzying, disorienting sensation he'd had the night before. He put out a hand and grasped the back of a chair to steady himself.

After he took several deep breaths, Jeffrey's head stopped swimming. Resolutely, he stood up straight and concentrated on getting to the job. He grabbed a pair of work gloves and headed for the door. He was about to leave his room when he saw the message light flashing on his answering machine.

With a stab of guilt Jeffrey remembered that he hadn't called Barbara the night before. He should have been thinking about Barbara just now, not Rebecca. Jeffrey pressed the button and listened to the tape.

"Hi, Jeffrey, it's Barbara. I fell asleep really early. I guess this dumb answering machine of mine is broken again, because I didn't get your message. Call me when you get home from your moving job, okay? I love you. Bye."

Jeffrey pushed the button again to rewind the tape. It was just one forgotten phone call. No big deal. Barbara would understand.

Jeffrey sighed. That was why he felt so guilty. Because Barbara would understand. And Barbara would forgive.

In what passed for downtown Winthrop, Miranda Stevens crossed her brown legs and leaned back in her chair. She pushed herself away from the desk which contained neat piles of paper. She rolled her chair back. It was mid-morning, and the first time the phones had stopped ringing.

Miranda crossed her arms behind her head and stared at the ceiling. Helping to run her mother's party planning and catering business was not her idea of the perfect summer job. But her mother needed the help in the summer, and the price was right.

The summer people gave lots of parties, and they had money to pay for them.

Miranda sighed. When she started college, though, she was going to put her foot down. She would find a summer job that would help her in her career. Whatever that was. Of all her friends only Jeffrey knew what he was going to do.

The phone rang. Here comes another party, she thought as she answered the phone. "Partyplanner. How can I help you?"

"Hi, Miranda. It's Barbara."

"Hey, what's up?"

"Well, you'll never guess. You know the new hair salon in the mall? It's always booked up, but I've been on a waiting list. They just called me and told me they have a cancellation."

"Uh-huh." Miranda could hear the bubbling enthusiasm in Barbara's voice.

"They can take me if I can get over there right away. I want to surprise Jeffrey with my new hairstyle tonight."

Miranda blinked. "What do you mean, 'new hairstyle'? Dozens of girls would *kill* for hair like yours. What are you going to do?"

"It's a surprise," Barbara said brightly. "There's only one problem, Miranda."

"What's that?"

"Mrs. Thomas has to run some errands, and I told her I'd stay with Tony for a while."

"Well, you know I can't leave all these parties waiting to happen. I'm glued to this desk."

"I know, I know," Barbara said in an agonized voice. "I thought maybe you could think of something. Any ideas?"

"No, not a one," Miranda replied, tapping her fingers on the desk. "Frankly, this could be a blessing in disguise. You shouldn't do a thing to your hair."

As soon as the words were out of her mouth, Miranda saw someone pass by the window from a corner of her eye. There was a sweep of long black hair.

Rebecca!

"Hang on, Barbara," Miranda said, putting the phone on the desk as she got to her feet. "If I'm lucky, your problem is solved." She hurried outside, yelling, "Rebecca! Rebecca, wait! I've got to ask you something!"

Later that morning, Mrs. Ada Cary set off as usual on her daily routine. As always, she took the route that led past the Thomas house, where the boy Tony was usually playing in the front yard.

Today Tony wasn't playing out front. From the street Mrs. Cary could see Tony in the backyard, right by the Thomases' garden. There was someone with him.

Mrs. Cary recognized the extraordinary girl she'd seen drive into town in the red convertible. Even in the black shirt and black cutoff shorts she was wearing, she was exquisite.

What a funny coincidence, thought Mrs. Cary. She'd seen the girl drive through town a short while ago, and now here she was. It wasn't the first time she'd seen her at the Thomas house, either. No, the girl was around more and more.

Hypnotized by Rebecca's magnetic presence, Mrs. Cary drew closer. Soon she was only a few feet from the backyard fence. There she stood in silence, watching the breathtakingly beautiful girl and the young boy.

But the longer Mrs. Cary stood there, the more wary she became. She prided herself on her feelings about people. She called it her "second sight."

Mrs. Cary sensed something about this girl that was *wrong*. She didn't know why, but the girl made her feel afraid.

Mrs. Cary's eyes narrowed. The wrongness was an aura around the girl. She could see that now. She was going to march right down to Mr. Thomas's hardware store and tell him he should never let this girl stay with Tony. Mr. Thomas would listen to her, too.

After all, she'd been his first-grade teacher.

Suddenly, the girl in the backyard looked up sharply, and stared right at Mrs. Cary. Mrs. Cary could feel the girl's eyes boring into her own.

Slowly, Mrs. Cary began backing away, step after faltering step. The girl stared steadily at her, with a look so cold, so full of unearthly fury, it sent an icy chill of fear into her heart. When she finally made it to the edge of the yard, Mrs. Cary turned around unsteadily and began walking away, toward Mr. Thomas's store. Her heart was beating rapidly.

Mrs. Cary hadn't gone very far when she felt the first sting. It was a quick, sharp, stab — like a bee sting. A searing pain surged through her leg and she drew her breath in with a gasp of hurt and surprise.

She waved her hand, to shoo away the bee. As she did, she felt another sting on her neck. It was followed by a white-hot flash of pain. Frantically, Mrs. Cary swatted at the bee. And then she felt another sting.

Just then, Mrs. Donnelly, the Thomases' next-door neighbor, happened to look out the front window. She saw Mrs. Cary and shook her head. The poor old lady is getting stranger and stranger, she thought. A few years ago, she started telling people about her "second sight." Now here she was, waving her hands and hopping around on the sidewalk. Goodness knows what she thought she was doing. Mrs. Donnelly shook her head again, and went back to reading her magazine.

By then, panic had seized control of Mrs. Cary. The stings came faster and faster, each one followed by terrible pain. The merciless bees were stinging her all over. Mrs. Cary waved her hands wildly.

She tried to scream, but couldn't make a sound. The bees made a frightening noise that grew louder and louder. It wasn't the buzzing sound of ordinary bees, but a menacing hiss, like snakes.

Mrs. Cary fell to the ground, no longer able to even try to defend herself from the angry swarm that stung her again and again and again.

The most terrifying thing was that while she felt the horrible stinging, she hadn't seen a single bee.

Chapter 11

The sidewalks shimmered in the early afternoon heat. Jeffrey took a bandana out of his pocket and mopped his brow.

Today's moving job had been one of the toughest ever. Plus, Mr. Smeal hadn't let up on him for being late. But now it was over. Jeffrey sat down on a packing crate on the front lawn and lifted a cold soda to his lips.

"Don't gulp," Paul said, sitting down next to him. His wiry black hair was dotted with beads of sweat.

Jeffrey took several long swallows of soda. Then he took a deep breath and let it out in a quick burst. "I can't believe this job is over."

"Neither can I. I can't believe Mr. Smeal stopped yelling at you, either." Paul grinned. " 'You're late! You're late! You're late!' " He said in a singsong imitation of Mr. Smeal.

Jeffrey shook his head. "He flies off the handle, all right."

"Hey," Paul said, giving Jeffrey a nudge. "Take a look over there in the car. There's somebody who's trying to get your attention."

Jeffrey looked toward the street and saw that, indeed, there was a girl waving at him from her car. She had stopped at the light.

Jeffrey kept looking at the girl while his mind tried to connect bits of information that didn't fit. It was as if he were trying to put together pieces from different puzzles. He kept trying, but it just wouldn't work. The world had tilted.

He knew the girl in the car. She just didn't look like the girl he knew. The girl in the car didn't look like Barbara. *But it was.*

Barbara's hair had been cut . . . off. Her hair was cut in a severe, close-cropped style that hugged her head. The style gave her features a completely different look.

"Jeffrey, I'm so glad I happened to run into you. Do you like my haircut?" Barbara called, smiling.

Jeffrey got up off the packing case and took a slow walk toward Barbara's car. What in the world had made her chop off those gorgeous red curls? he wondered. He hoped she hadn't seen the shock on his face. As he got closer,

Jeffrey could see that Barbara was wearing all black clothes. The whole effect was jarring.

"Well, what do you think of my haircut, Jeffrey?" Barbara asked again.

The light changed, and a man in the car behind Barbara's honked the horn. "Hey, let's get going *today*," he yelled out.

"Go on, I'll call you later," Jeffrey called to her.

Barbara stepped on the gas and was gone. Jeffrey stared after the car. When it had vanished from sight, he walked back to where Paul still sat on the packing case.

"Paul, did you see that?" Jeffrey asked.

"*That* being Barbara?"

"I'm talking about Barbara's haircut."

"Well, yeah. It's hard to miss. She looks different, all right."

Later that day, Jeffrey arrived home to an empty house. There was a note on the dining room table.

I've taken Tony out for ice cream. Rebecca.

Rebecca? Why had she been here? Jeffrey threw the note down on the table.

Why was Rebecca always around? he wondered. She was always turning up at Sharkey's. She and Barbara spent lots of time

74

together. Or she just "happened to be passing by."

After a moment, Jeffrey realized his teeth were clenched tightly. He relaxed, surprised at his sudden surge of annoyance.

What's the big deal if Rebecca was always around? he asked himself. She was nice enough. Everybody liked her. So why should he care?

I don't care, Jeffrey told himself. He decided to call Barbara. His hand was on the telephone when it rang.

"Hello?" Jeffrey half expected it to be Barbara. He was surprised to hear his father's voice.

"Jeffrey, what happened to you today?" Mr. Thomas's voice crackled through the telephone. He sounded exasperated.

"What do you mean?"

"You don't know what I mean? I can't believe it." Now Mr. Thomas sounded just plain angry. "You never stopped by the store to pick up the cash. Now the bank's closed and I'll have to keep it all here overnight."

"Oh! I don't know how I forgot." Jeffrey slumped in a chair, cradling the phone next to his ear, as recollection set in.

How, indeed, had he forgotten?

"I don't know where your mind was." Mr. Thomas ranted on. "Besides — I saw you drive by here twice today. I even ran out into the street and tried to flag you down."

It was true. After the moving job, Jeffrey had cruised around aimlessly before coming home. He couldn't remember what he'd been thinking about.

"It won't happen again," Jeffrey assured his father. He couldn't think of anything else to say.

After he hung up, Jeffrey paced the floor. Every summer for the past couple of years almost every day he'd stopped at his father's store and taken a bag of cash to the bank. If a moving job ran late he called so his father could make other arrangements to get the cash to the bank. Jeffrey had done the errand so many times it was automatic. But not today.

The front door opened, and Tony came running into the room. He was wearing bright red overalls and a yellow T-shirt. Behind him was Mrs. Thomas, dressed in jeans and a white cotton top.

"What happened to Rebecca?" Jeffrey asked. "I saw a note from her."

"She stayed with Tony while I did some errands," Mrs. Thomas answered. "I saw her coming out of Abbott's with Tony as I was coming down the street, so I picked him up and told her to go on home."

"Oh." Jeffrey pushed away a twinge of disappointment, denying that he felt it at all.

"Rebecca and I played in the backyard all afternoon," Tony said with a big smile.

"That's good." Jeffrey patted Tony on the shoulder.

Jeffrey's mother tossed some packages onto the dining room table. "I stopped into Abbott's myself, and Mr. Abbott told me the strangest thing." She turned to Jeffrey. "One of the neighbors told him that Mrs. Cary was taken to the hospital in an ambulance. She was covered with insect bites — as if she'd been attacked by a swarm of bees."

Jeffrey didn't know what to make of the information. "That *is* really odd. I've never heard of anything like that happening around here."

"I know. It's so strange. Poor Mrs. Cary." Mrs. Thomas picked up a bag of peaches and carried them into the kitchen.

"I promised Barbara I'd phone her," Jeffrey said, more to remind himself than to tell anyone else. He wasn't going to forget to call Barbara again.

"Before you make the call, could you do me a favor?" Mrs. Thomas came back into the dining room, wiping her hands on her jeans. "Would you go out back and get something for a salad from the garden?"

"Sure thing."

Jeffrey headed out through the kitchen. He thought he'd pick a few tomatoes and maybe dig up some carrots. Letting the screen door slam behind him, he bounded down the porch steps and into the yard. He hoped the tomatoes were ripe enough. He whistled as he walked.

But as Jeffrey neared the garden, he fell silent, and slowed his pace.

Something was horribly, horribly wrong. Only a day or two before, he had come out to the garden to check the tomato plants. The tomatoes had been plump and juicy, just a shade away from being at the peak of ripeness. Now the plants were brown and withered, the leaves curled and shriveled, so brittle that they broke apart when he touched them. The rotten tomatoes had fallen to the ground and smashed apart. They gave off the sickening stench of decay. Worms were crawling through them.

Jeffrey looked at the carrots next. Their leafy tops were dried up, too. He squatted down and dug one out of the dirt. It was dry as a twig.

Jeffrey saw a line of red ants marching along

the parched earth, carrying bits of rotted plants and vegetables. He stood up and scuffed his toe lightly in the dirt, and a tiny puff of dust flew up.

Jeffrey saw that the rosebushes near the garden were dried up, too. The withered petals of the once beautiful, fragrant flowers lay scattered on the ground.

Jeffrey looked around the garden in shock and disbelief. It was as if some force had drawn all the life from it.

The last time he'd looked at the garden it had been bursting with health. Now there was only death and decay.

Chapter 12

It was Saturday, another day of merciless, suffocating heat. The sun blazed like a fiery ball in the sky.

Miranda Stevens hurried into the Parfumerie, sighing with relief as the cool air inside caressed her burning skin. She pulled at her damp shirt where it was stuck to her midriff.

She and Barbara were meeting at the store and spending the afternoon together. It had been three days since Barbara had gotten her hair cut, but this was the first time Miranda would see it.

A feeling of apprehension tightened Miranda's stomach. She had an idea that she wouldn't like what she would see. Paul had seen the haircut and told Miranda about it. He had used words like "unusual," "different," and "striking." He never said Barbara's haircut looked bad — but he never said it looked good, either.

Paul was very diplomatic. It probably meant Barbara's hair looked awful.

Miranda looked around the store. There were rows upon rows of scented powders, lotions, shampoos, and soaps. The air was full of scents. The merchandise was a rainbow of colors — pink, yellow, and green lotions; pale amber and ivory shampoos; blue-and-cream colored bottles of powder.

The clerk, Miranda could tell, wasn't thrilled to be working at the Parfumerie. Tall and lanky, with glasses that kept sliding down his thin nose, he did little to disguise his discontent. He sighed with boredom as he rang up a sale, and curled his lip in a grimace when someone asked for help.

The clerk was adept at avoiding the customers. When another person asked for assistance, he pretended he hadn't heard, and disappeared into the stockroom.

Miranda crossed her arms and watched the clerk. I'd straighten him right out, she said to herself. I wouldn't let him get away with the disappearing act.

But Miranda didn't want the clerk's help. She wasn't looking for something to buy. She was only there to meet Barbara.

The bell over the door tinkled as the door opened. Miranda was surprised to see Rebecca enter. Her willowy figure was clothed in a simple black summer dress with thin straps. Her bare skin gleamed like creamy ivory. Miranda noticed how vibrant she looked — how light and cool.

Without looking right or left, Rebecca walked through the store and stepped up to the perfume counter. Although she didn't pay the slightest attention to the other people in the store, they noticed her. Many of them stared openly. Rebecca was unruffled.

Miranda looked on with fascination as the effect of Rebecca's presence flashed through the room. The clerk came out from the stockroom and walked instantly to Rebecca. Instead of a sullen expression, his face was transformed by a wide smile. "May I help you?" He asked, sounding eager. He looked at Rebecca as if to help her was what he lived for.

The whole thing is just amazing, thought Miranda as she looked at the scene. A tall, disgruntled-looking woman who'd been waiting for a long time and grumbling loudly about it grew red in the face when she saw the clerk helping Rebecca. The woman's lips formed in a determined line, and her chin jutted forward.

She opened her mouth to speak. Miranda watched as Rebecca turned toward the woman and inclined her head gracefully. Immediately, the woman closed her mouth and started backing away. The woman's manner had suddenly become timid. She practically shrank in size.

As Rebecca gave instructions to the clerk, he quickly began mixing together liquids from different vials. He was creating a scent just for her.

Miranda heard the bell over the door jingle again. This time Barbara came in. Miranda took one look at her and was stunned.

Barbara was wearing a black dress much like the one Rebecca had on. Her hair was about an inch long and was sprayed flat to her head.

On someone else the severe hairstyle might have been flattering — but not on Barbara. Her hair was so gorgeous, and now it's gone, Miranda thought. The cut makes Barbara look like a little boy. And that *dress*. It doesn't suit Barbara at all.

Then Miranda saw something that startled her even more. Barbara, who never wore nail polish, had painted her nails red.

While Miranda was trying to recover from the effects of Barbara's appearance, Rebecca looked straight ahead, and said, "Barbara."

But she couldn't have known it was Barbara. Rebecca's back was toward the entrance to the store. It was as if she had sensed Barbara was there.

Rebecca turned around, her face lit up with a look of delight. "Barbara!" she exclaimed. "You look wonderful! That haircut really brings out your eyes. And the dress!" Rebecca paused to walk around Barbara in a complete circle. Then she announced, "That dress is perfect."

It looks perfectly awful, Miranda thought. Rebecca couldn't possibly think Barbara looked wonderful. Yet there was Rebecca, exclaiming over Barbara, looking as if she believed every word. A hard grain of suspicion lodged in Miranda's mind.

Rebecca paid for her purchase and tucked it into her purse. She turned back to Barbara. "It was so nice to see you," she said in her silvery voice. "We'll have to get together soon. Maybe you and Jeffrey can both come over."

The fact that Jeffrey was included in the invitation was not lost on Miranda. Rebecca had quite a slick routine, she thought, taking in Rebecca's engaging smile and Barbara's expression of rapt attention.

With scarcely a glance at Miranda as she said good-bye, Rebecca turned and glided toward the door. The people in the store stared at her with undisguised fascination.

When Rebecca was gone, the atmosphere in the store returned to normal. The tall woman that Rebecca had silenced with a glance began complaining again. The clerk's smile drooped into a frown. Once again, he disappeared into the stockroom.

Barbara turned to Miranda and asked brightly, "Do you like my haircut?"

Miranda hesitated before she spoke. She didn't want to hurt Barbara's feelings. But it just wasn't in her to lie. "The style is certainly fashionable," she said after a moment.

Barbara took Miranda's statement as a compliment.

"Thanks," she said.

"How does Jeffrey like your haircut?" Miranda asked. She watched Barbara stiffen slightly.

"Oh, he likes it a lot," Barbara said, too forcefully. She looked at Miranda. "What did Rebecca buy?"

Miranda shrugged. "I don't know. Some scent the clerk made up specially for her."

Barbara looked disappointed. "Oh. Too bad. I would have gotten the same one." Then her face brightened. "Do you think he'll remember what he mixed up for her?"

Miranda was taken aback. "Barbara, why would you want to wear the same perfume as Rebecca?"

Now that Miranda had gotten started, she couldn't stop voicing her concern. "What's come over you, Barbara? You're dressing like Rebecca, wearing the same kind of clothes, the same color nail polish. You're always talking about looking sophisticated. You say that word, 'sophisticated,' almost as often as you say Rebecca's name."

When Barbara spoke, her green eyes flashed defiantly. "Why shouldn't I try to be like Rebecca. She's fantastic! What do you think is wrong with Rebecca?"

Miranda looked at Barbara, shocked at her friend's words. She couldn't imagine Barbara wanting to be just like someone else. It wasn't like Barbara at all.

"Well," Barbara persisted, "what's *wrong* with Rebecca?"

Miranda stared back at Barbara, unable to answer her. This conversation isn't going anywhere, she thought. "Never mind, Barbara," she said.

"You started this, so don't tell me 'never mind,'" Barbara shot back in a defiant tone. Her eyes flashed with anger.

Miranda was silent for a moment. She searched for the right words to express the way she felt. "Have you noticed the way things have changed around here since Rebecca arrived?" Miranda looked at Barbara. She was staring back at her with an uncomprehending look. "Rebecca is the kiss of death," she said, finally.

"The kiss of death," echoed Barbara. "That's crazy," she said with a dismissive wave of her hand. She found Miranda's statement so amusing that she wasn't angry anymore. "The kiss of death," she repeated, chuckling.

Later that night, the fog rolled in again. Miranda and Barbara met Paul and Jeffrey at Sharkey's.

As she watched Jeffrey and Barbara together, the uncomfortable feeling Miranda had had started to grow stronger and stronger. Jeffrey and Barbara weren't behaving in their usual way. There was a subtle difference, something Miranda couldn't explain — but they were strangely out of sync.

If Miranda could have read Jeffrey's mind,

she would have known he felt the same way she did. He found Barbara so different he almost felt he was with someone he didn't know.

What made Jeffrey even more uncomfortable was that when he looked at Barbara dressed in black, with her nails painted red, it reminded him constantly of Rebecca. It filled him with a jumble of confusing sensations.

By the end of the evening Miranda was sure that something was very wrong. Jeffrey and Barbara had changed, and there was something eerie about the way they had changed.

They were distracted, uncomfortable, and Miranda felt that when Jeffrey looked at Barbara he was seeing a dark-haired girl with violet eyes.

Chapter 13

As the days went by, people wondered when the break in the heat would come. It seemed as if the strange parade of stifling hot days followed by nights thick with fog would go on and on forever.

Jeffrey and Paul were going home from another moving job in Jeffrey's car. They were covered with dirt and sweat.

"Thank goodness you have a car with air-conditioning," Paul said, bending down to loosen the laces on his work boots.

"When do you get your car out of the shop?" Jeffrey asked.

"In a few days. They have to put in a new muffler. It's going to cost me a couple of hundred bucks."

"That's rough."

Paul sighed audibly. "Tell me about it." He sat up straighter. "Hey, Jeffrey, check this out. You know my mother's a nurse at Winthrop Hospital, right?"

Jeffrey nodded.

"Well, about a week and a half ago, they brought in an old lady who'd been stung all over by insects."

"I know. It was one of our neighbors, Mrs. Cary. She was attacked by a swarm of bees."

Paul shook his head. "Nah, that's not it. At first they *thought* it was bees. But when the doctors started examining the lady, they said that whatever stung her, it wasn't bees. In fact, it couldn't have been any kind of insect that lives in this part of the country."

"Really?" Jeffrey frowned thoughtfully. "That's weird. What kind of insects were they?"

Paul spoke in a hushed voice. "It's weird all right. And it gets weirder. They brought in a specialist — some kind of expert — and he said he'd never seen anything like the welts the lady had, or the marks made by the stingers. He said whatever attacked the lady was some kind of insect he didn't know existed."

Jeffrey's eyebrows shot up. "That's amazing."

"Yeah," Paul went on. "And that's not all." His big hands gripped his knees. "The lady who got bitten is getting better, but since she arrived at the hospital, she hasn't been able to say a word."

Jeffrey tightened his grip on the steering wheel. "That's really, really strange. There was never anything the matter with Mrs. Cary's voice. She always talked a lot, as a matter of fact."

Paul shrugged. "Well, she's not talking now. I'll tell you something — I'm going to be on the lookout for bugs."

"Good idea." Jeffrey made the turn onto Paul's street.

"Thanks for the lift," Paul said as Jeffrey pulled in front of his house.

"No problem. See you later. We're still on for the Jazz Joint, right?"

"You bet. It's gonna be great," Paul said, getting out of the car. "Wait till you hear this group." He leaned down to speak to Jeffrey. "Just pick me up by seven-thirty, okay? This group always opens right on time, and I don't want to be late."

"You've got it. Seven-thirty. I'll be here." Jeffrey eased his car onto the road.

As he drove, Jeffrey moved his muscular shoulders in small circles, trying to stretch a little. The moving job shouldn't have been difficult that day, but in the heat it had been murder.

Besides, Jeffrey felt a little out of it. He hadn't had a good night's sleep for several days now. Either he'd toss and turn, unable to get to sleep, or wake from a nightmare in the middle of the night, breathing hard and sweating.

Well, it won't help to worry about it, he told himself. But he *was* worried.

Jeffrey looked out at the trees, and the white clouds that dotted the blue sky overhead. He decided to go for a drive to the ocean.

As he drove, Jeffrey began to feel better. Gradually, he found a feeling of comfort creeping into his body. He felt a tide of relaxation washing over him. He took a deep breath. It was as if a soothing balm was enveloping him inside and out.

Jeffrey soon felt completely peaceful and clearheaded. He glanced out at the white clouds overhead. He had the sensation that his body was getting lighter and lighter, until he was floating along with the clouds in the sky. He felt euphoric.

Then suddenly, everything changed. There was a noise singing in his ears. Soft at first, then louder and more insistent. Jeffrey pressed a hand to his forehead. It was like no noise he'd ever heard.

He wanted to put both hands over his ears

to block out the terrible sound, but, of course, he couldn't let go of the steering wheel. Even more terrifying than the noise was the realization that he couldn't shut out the noise anyway, because it was coming from somewhere deep inside his head. He drove on blindly, paying no attention to where he was going.

Then, darkly frightening, a black haze began to envelop him. First it crept in from the edges of his vision, but soon it completely clouded his sight so that he could see nothing but a black void. Jeffrey began falling into the emptiness with tremendous speed. It was sucking him in and smothering him. He wanted to scream, but he could get no air into his lungs.

He couldn't tell how fast the car was going anymore. He tried to keep his head, slow down, and pull over, without knowing where he was going. Jeffrey waited for the crash he knew would come. He couldn't see or hear anymore . . . and he was beginning to forget who he was.

Jeffrey made a last desperate attempt to hold onto a thread of awareness. Then there was only darkness.

Chapter 14

The same afternoon that Jeffrey took his terrifying drive out toward the cliffs overlooking the ocean, Rebecca Webster also decided to go for a ride. As she rode along in her shiny red convertible, her glistening ruby lips were curved in a wide smile. From the look on her face, whatever she was thinking pleased her very much. The crimson nails on her slender, tapered fingers sparkled in the sun as she gripped the steering wheel. She drove slowly, so that instead of whipping out behind her, her hair moved softly about her shoulders.

As Rebecca passed other cars, the drivers stared and had to force themselves to look back at the road. She drove past a construction site, but received no whistles, catcalls, or raucous remarks. Instead, every guy stopped working and gazed at her with longing.

Rebecca didn't glance at the construction

workers. She stared straight ahead, an enigmatic smile fixed on her lips, thinking her private thoughts.

Though her speed was leisurely, her route wasn't aimless. Rebecca always knew exactly where she was going.

As she neared her destination, she pressed her slim foot, encased in a soft black leather boot, down on the gas pedal. As the car sped up, Rebecca's eyes narrowed slightly and the lights inside them leaped like flames.

Jeffrey sat up sharply and blinked. He was completely disoriented. He had absolutely no idea where he was, or how he'd gotten there.

He turned his head from side to side and looked around. There were trees on either side of him. Jeffrey climbed out of the car and walked around it in a circle, checking for signs of damage. There wasn't even a scratch.

Jeffrey wished that he, too, was fine. But he had to walk slowly to avoid losing his balance. Every few steps, his vision blurred and he felt dizzy. His whole body felt as if he had fallen down and slammed into the ground. He got back into the car, leaned his head back against the seat, and dozed.

When he woke up some time later, Jeffrey felt a little better. At least, he felt well enough to think about getting out of there.

Time. What time was it? Memory of his appointment with Paul flashed through his mind. Hurriedly, he looked at his watch. It was almost quarter to seven.

Jeffrey sat upright. He'd have to figure out where he was in a hurry, and how to get to Paul's from wherever he was by seven-thirty. There was no time to lose.

Great. Just great, Jeffrey said to himself. He probably wouldn't have time to take a shower. He wondered if they'd even let him in the club looking the way he did. Jeffrey glanced down at his work-soiled T-shirt and muttered, "Ugh."

Things went from bad to worse. Jeffrey turned the key in the ignition, but the car didn't start. He tried again. Still nothing. He gritted his teeth and tried a third time. Nothing happened. Then he noticed the "gas" light blinking, and slapped the steering wheel. The car was out of gas.

Now I'll be lucky if I get to Paul's at all, Jeffrey thought. He got out of the car. There was an empty gas can in the trunk. Jeffrey got it and started walking.

Rebecca's smile widened as she turned onto the narrow dirt road that wound into the woods. It led to a cemetery that no one visited anymore.

The entrance to the road was overgrown with weeds. No one would have noticed it unless they looked closely, but Rebecca located it instantly. She turned without hesitation, for she had been down the road before.

As Jeffrey saw the raven-haired girl in the gleaming red convertible coming toward him on the dirt road, his eyes widened. Rebecca's beautiful face betrayed not the slightest trace of surprise.

"Rebecca," Jeffrey said incredulously, as the car drove alongside.

"Hello, Jeffrey." Rebecca looked deep into his eyes.

"I'm so glad to see you! I must've blacked out — and when I came to I had no idea where I was. And my car's out of gas."

Rebecca studied Jeffrey's face. "You look a little shaken up. And you look a little tired, too. Maybe it's the heat."

"Maybe you're right. Paul and I were working outside a lot today. The heat doesn't seem to be bothering you, though." It was true. Jeffrey looked at Rebecca and thought how amazingly fresh she looked, as if she'd stepped out of a cool breeze.

"Anyway," Jeffrey went on, "it's strange to run into you out here. What are you doing on this road?"

Looking steadily at Jeffrey, Rebecca replied, "It's where I discovered the cemetery you saw in my painting. I think I may do another picture of it. I find it so . . . interesting."

Memories of the night Jeffrey had gone to see Rebecca's painting came flooding back. The image of her bathed in candlelight floated into his mind. He pushed the vision away.

Rebecca loked up at Jeffrey, and for a moment he felt himself drowning in the violet depths of her eyes. He could only stand and stare.

"Get in the car, Jeffrey," Rebecca said finally. "There must be somewhere that you want to go."

Jeffrey opened the car door and got inside. "I need to get to a gas station."

Rebecca stared straight ahead. "Let's go."

The dirt road was so narrow that Rebecca had to back up the convertible all the way to the end. "I see where we are now," Jeffrey said as they turned onto the highway. "I can't imagine what made me turn down that side road."

Rebecca glanced at Jeffrey, acknowledging his remark. The sun cast flickering golden sparkles of light in her eyes. "You've checked your watch four times. You must be in a hurry," she remarked after they'd driven a short while.

Jeffrey told her about his seven-thirty appointment with Paul. Rebecca listened without comment.

"What are you doing?" Jeffrey said suddenly, as Rebecca flew past a gas station without slowing down.

"I'm driving you to Paul's house," Rebecca said with a tone of finality in her voice. "You'll never make it by seven-thirty if you go to a gas station and then back to your car."

"That's very thoughtful of you, Rebecca," he said after a moment. "Let me show you where Paul lives."

Rebecca shook her head, tossing her tangle of shimmering hair. "I know where Paul lives."

"Really? I'm surprised . . ." Jeffrey's voice trailed off. Then he said, "I don't want to put you to any trouble." He watched the way the sun caressed Rebecca's face, making her skin glow.

"Don't worry about it." Rebecca glanced sideways at Jeffrey, from under her dark lashes. "Maybe you can clean up at Paul's, and he can lend you a shirt."

"Good idea." Jeffrey remembered how dirty he was.

"Anyway," Rebecca went on in her silvery voice, "I'm not doing this favor for free." A mysterious smile played about Rebecca's lips. "I hope there's a favor you'll do for me in return."

Jeffrey sat up straighter. "What did you have in mind?"

Rebecca ran her tapered fingers along the steering wheel. When she spoke, her voice was hushed, but pulsed with energy. "I want to try painting portraits. I need someone to sit for me, to be a model."

Jeffrey stared at Rebecca, at her ivory, satin skin, masses of ebony hair. Her plain black T-shirt and jeans clung to her body. She was breathtakingly beautiful.

Jeffrey swallowed hard. If he agreed to sit for Rebecca, they'd be spending hours alone together. He didn't want to be alone for hours with her. The skin on the back of his neck tingled at the thought.

"All right," he said, not knowing why he didn't refuse.

Chapter 15

"It just sounds *too* perfect." Miranda Stevens hugged her knees to her chest. She and Paul were sitting on the floor of her rec room. There was a steady beat of music in the background.

Paul shook his head. "I think the way Rebecca showed up last night to get us to the club was great. Period. If she hadn't happened by to rescue Jeffrey from car trouble, we probably never would have made it to the club at all." He turned on his side and rested his chin on his hand. "It was pretty nice of her to take us to the show."

Miranda looked thoughtful. "Did Rebecca stay for the show, by any chance?"

"Of course she did," said Paul, watching Miranda's face. "Naturally, we offered to take her with us. After she'd volunteered to drive us there, what else were we going to do?"

Miranda nodded slowly. "I figured something like that."

Paul sat up straight and stretched his long legs, clad in faded jeans, out in front of him. "I don't know what you're getting at, Miranda," he said slowly. "I admit that I didn't understand why everybody was going nuts about Rebecca. I still don't. But I do know this. Rebecca is a really nice girl, and I think she needs friends."

Miranda got to her feet and crossed her arms. As she spoke, she walked back and forth across the floor. "There's something weird about the way Rebecca *just happened* by when Jeffrey was in trouble. And that she *just happened* to end up spending the evening with him."

"With both of us."

Miranda stood still and tilted her head to one side. "Okay. But haven't you noticed how many coincidences throw Rebecca and Jeffrey together?" She started pacing the floor again. "Here's something else I wonder about. Practically every guy in town is falling all over himself to go out with Rebecca. But she never dates anybody. I think the only guy she's interested in being around is Jeffrey."

Paul looked down and rubbed one hand on

his knee. "I don't think you can presume that," he said quietly.

For several moments there was silence in the room. Miranda kept looking at Paul. "Hey, why did you clam up all of a sudden?"

Without saying a word, Paul started flipping through a pile of CD's on the floor beside him.

"I knew it," Miranda sat down on the floor beside Paul. She took his chin in her hand and turned his face toward hers. "There *is* something you're not telling me. What is it?"

Paul looked at the ceiling for a moment. Then he looked back at Miranda. "Look," he said firmly. "There *is* something I didn't tell you because I knew you'd make a big deal out of it, and I don't think it's a big deal at all."

Miranda kept looking at him without saying a word.

"It's just that — well, Rebecca paints pictures — and she wants to try painting portraits. So Jeffrey is going to model for her." Paul got the last words out very quickly.

Miranda's eyes grew wider and wider. "Oh, come on, Paul!" she said incredulously. "You don't really believe she wants Jeffrey to sit for a portrait! If you do, that girl has made you lose your good sense, just like everyone else around here."

Paul gave a halfhearted shrug. "See, I knew you'd make a big thing out of it. She helped Jeffrey out, and he's just returning the favor."

With a dismissive wave of her hand, Miranda said, "That's the most gullible kind of statement I've ever heard from you. I guess Rebecca's got you brainwashed after all."

After Paul left, Miranda couldn't stop thinking about what he'd told her. She almost phoned Barbara to talk about Jeffrey's role in Rebecca's new art project, but stopped short just as she was about to make the call. It wasn't the first time Miranda had stopped herself from saying something to Barbara about Rebecca. Every time she started to speak, she remembered Barbara's fierce admiration for Rebecca, and held her tongue. Barbara probably would just get angry at any suggestion that Rebecca was doing something underhanded.

For a while Miranda tried forgetting about the whole situation. She told herself it was none of her business. But she just couldn't let it rest.

An hour after Paul had gone home, Miranda was getting into her car, her mind set on driving out to the cliffs where Rebecca lived. She had no idea what she'd do when she got there, but she felt compelled to go. She had to find something out that would convince Barbara that Rebecca wasn't the wonderful friend she thought her to be.

Miranda had no idea how she would find the evidence of Rebecca's dishonesty. But she had to try.

When Miranda left the house, the sky had just gotten dark. As she turned onto the highway that led toward the road up the cliffs, the night was clear. Miranda could see stars twinkling in the sky.

It took about an hour to drive from the section of Winthrop where Miranda lived to the cliffs overlooking the sea. Miranda had driven about halfway when the mist started collecting on the car windshield.

Here we go again with this crazy weather, she thought. She frowned. Probably something to do with the ozone layer, Miranda said to herself. She wished she believed it was that simple. There was something unsettling about the weather this summer, something too strange to be explained by environmental factors.

The further Miranda drove, the thicker the mist got. By the time she neared the cliffs, it had turned into fog that rolled around the trees and draped itself over the rocks like a glowing shroud.

It's much too warm for fog like this, Miranda thought, watching the way it moved, curling through the air. There's something sinister about it.

The fog reflected the light from the car's headlights, causing a glare in Miranda's eyes. Common sense told her to turn around, but she ignored what her mind told her and drove on. Soon she was close to the dirt road she knew led to Rebecca's house. There was only one house, and only one road to it, on the cliffs.

Miranda pulled alongside the road. Should I turn, and go on to Rebecca's house? she wondered. What then? What should I do?

Miranda started to turn the steering wheel, to send the car down the dirt road. Her mind wavered. And then she saw something that sent her soul rising into her throat.

There was a creature wandering in the woods, a creature with a face that reflected the moonlight like polished marble. A creature whose huge eyes glittered with unearthly life. Miranda sat paralyzed as she gazed at something not of this world.

The creature floated among the trees, moving this way and that as if hypnotized. It was the most haunting vision Miranda had ever seen.

And then she realized it was Rebecca.

Chapter 16

It was Rebecca, but not the vibrant, seductive Rebecca of daylight. This Rebecca burned with the fire of night, the fire of darkness. The glow of her skin was a ghostly radiance. Her large eyes glittered with a strange and terrifying light.

Rebecca's shimmering hair tangled wildly around her face. She wore a flowing, filmy black dress that blended with the night. As she walked in the woods the mists curled around her, caressing her. As she moved she floated in the fog, almost as if her feet didn't touch the ground.

So shocking was Rebecca's appearance that for several moments Miranda lost awareness of anything but the haunting vision. She even forgot to breathe. It was only when she began feeling lightheaded that Miranda's body took over and involuntarily she drew in great gasps of air. Her heart hammered wildly.

Unable to take her eyes from the specter of Rebecca, Miranda watched as she wandered in the woods. Rebecca moved as if in a trance, slowly at times, and then with a startling violence of motion. She would stop sometimes, and remain as still as if she were sleeping, and then suddenly begin wandering again. Though her direction was aimless, she had the look of someone seeking something — something deep within herself.

What is she doing out here? Miranda wondered. Her presence in these woods couldn't possibly be for any normal purpose.

Perhaps when I tell Barbara what I've seen, she'll think twice about Rebecca, Miranda said to herself. There was definitely something very strange about this girl floating among the trees in the night. It proved to Miranda that the feeling that she'd grown to believe more and more was true. There was much more to Rebecca than anyone knew or understood. Something hiding behind that dazzling smile, the violet eyes, the red lips.

Rebecca's movements were so mesmerizing, so hypnotic, that Miranda felt her eyelids getting heavy. So were her arms and legs. She was growing drowsier and drowsier with each passing moment.

Rebecca began twirling around, her filmy black dress whirling around her. She whirled faster and faster, until her dress blurred into a plume of black smoke that enveloped her.

On the verge of falling asleep, Miranda sat up suddenly, and blinked her eyes. It was impossible, she knew — but she was sure that she had just seen Rebecca vanish into the fog.

And then the ghostly figure in black stopped whirling, and looked right at Miranda, straight into her eyes and down into her soul. Miranda felt herself swimming in the violet depths of those eyes. She was falling into them as if into a bottomless pit.

When Miranda came swimming out of the violet pit, the figure walking in the woods was gone. The moon had vanished behind a cloud.

Now Miranda knew what it felt like to have one's blood chilled. Suddenly the temperature had dropped drastically. There was freezing, unbearable cold.

The cold made Miranda's teeth chatter uncontrollably. It grabbed her heart with an icy hand.

Miranda wanted desperately to get away from that place. The cold was terrifying. It had a cruel, punishing presence of its own.

Then it vanished abruptly. But for some

time longer, Miranda's teeth chattered from fear. In an instant, she was drenched with sweat.

Confused, terrified feelings tumbled over each other in her mind. She heard the roar of the surf below the cliffs, looked around the dark shapes of the trees.

Clumsily, she turned the key in the ignition and started the car. That's when Miranda caught sight of the clock on the dashboard, and her heart stood still. She had felt that everything that had happened since she got to the cliffs and saw the figure in the woods had taken place within minutes. But the clock told her that it was after three o'clock in the morning.

Miranda felt as if she had fallen through a hole in the fabric of time. Did I fall asleep and dream the cold? she wondered. Her mind told her that it wasn't possible. But then, her mind was playing tricks on her. Miranda's heart fluttered.

The clock in the car must be broken, she thought wildly. That's it. Miranda looked at her watch, willing it to prove her right. It was not to be. Miranda's watch was slower than the clock in the car by two minutes.

Feeling nauseous, Miranda turned the car onto the highway. Why did I come out here at night in the first place? she asked herself as she headed for home. Somewhere in the back of her mind was a faded thought that there was something she had planned to tell Barbara. But try as she might, she couldn't remember what it was.

Chapter 17

Another week went by, and Winthrop remained in the punishing grip of heat. People whose destination normally took them through Winthrop detoured. None of the other surrounding towns suffered such excruciating temperatures. Many people had stopped talking about the heat at all. They couldn't explain it, but talking about the heat made them fearful.

Oblivious to the soaring temperatures, Rebecca Webster walked in her lilting way down the streets of Winthrop. She was a picture of cool serenity that was a jarring contrast to the appearance of the rest of the town's inhabitants. While everyone else wilted in the heat, Rebecca looked cool and fresh as if she'd just been unwrapped.

Today her flawless face wore a confident smile. It was noontime, and every second brought the appointed time with Jeffrey a little closer. Of course, they weren't supposed to meet until seven o'clock the following evening. But the time would pass quickly.

One corner of Rebecca's perfect mouth curved a little more as she recalled Jeffrey's surprise when she'd suggested they meet in the evening. But when she explained that she wanted to paint by candlelight, he hadn't objected. Rebecca's mouth curved still more. No, she thought. Jeffrey hadn't objected at all.

In a single, fluid motion that was a delight to the eye, Rebecca took a seat at a sidewalk cafe. A baby-faced waiter glanced out the window and did a double take. It had been so hot that no one had sat in the outdoor cafe in weeks. Instantly, he hurried outside to take Rebecca's order, wearing an eager-to-please expression that was so pronounced it was comical.

Rebecca ordered an iced coffee. But when the waiter came dashing over with it, she let it sit in front of her without taking a sip. She merely tapped her red nails against the frosty surface of the glass as she gazed out at the nearly empty streets.

There was not much to see, given the general inactivity. But the sight of a man behind a window caught her eye.

The man was seated behind an untidy desk strewn with papers, and he was talking on the telephone. Rebecca fastened her gaze on the man in a cool, unblinking stare.

At first Rebecca found him amusing. As he talked on the phone his face got redder and redder and his gestures became wilder and wilder. Then he jumped to his feet, moving his mouth around in his face as he spoke. From the looks of him, he was yelling very loudly at the person on the other end of the line.

Slowly, Rebecca's expression changed. It was as if a shadow cast from within had fallen across her face. In an instant, her violet eyes became as hard and unyielding as stone. Her red lips set in a grim line. The man did not amuse her anymore.

Anyone looking at Rebecca would have sensed her darkening mood. Moment by moment, her expression grew more menacing. In seconds, Rebecca's face was twisted into a look of merciless rage that was all the more frightening because she was so beautiful.

At the same exact moment, Jeffrey Thomas was at home, holding the telephone receiver away from his ear to reduce the volume of Mr. Smeal's screaming from hitting his eardrum. The sounds of Smeal's squawking went on and on, hanging in the air. Jeffrey tapped his foot impatiently. He had heard this kind of thing before.

"Mr. Smeal, you should calm down. It's not good for a person to get so excited all of the time." Jeffrey spoke into the telephone during a lull in the screaming. As soon as he got the words out, the yelling began again.

When Smeal stopped to take a breath, Jeffrey said, "I only asked for *one* evening off, because I have plans. Who would want to move in the evening anyway?" His statement provoked another outburst.

As Jeffrey listened, he nodded wearily. Mr. Smeal was telling him that it was none of his business when people wanted to move. And if Jeffrey didn't want to work when the work was there to be done, he could find himself another job.

Jeffrey leaned his chin on his hand and waited for Mr. Smeal to stop ranting and raving. If only I didn't need the money for college, he thought. One thing you had to say for Mr. Smeal, he paid a top wage. And that's about *all* you could say in Mr. Smeal's favor, Jeffrey thought.

"All right, all right, I'll be at the job tomorrow night," Jeffrey said, cutting into Mr.

Smeal's tirade. Like magic, the screaming stopped.

Jeffrey hung up and got his address book. He thumbed through it, looking for Rebecca's telephone number. He'd have to tell her that he wouldn't be able to come over tomorrow.

He paused, his hand on the telephone. He realized that he was hoping that Rebecca would want to reschedule their appointment for some time soon. The awareness of it was like a sudden jolt.

Slowly, Jeffrey lowered himself into a chair. He was still holding the telephone. His eyes had a glazed expression as he searched his thoughts.

How long had he felt this way, and not known it? he wondered. This shouldn't happen, he told himself. I'm in love with Barbara. I was only going to Rebecca's house to do her a favor.

The image of Barbara's face floated before his mind's eye. He saw her sparkling green eyes and her sweet, gentle smile. And then the picture was blotted out by a vision of Rebecca.

Jeffrey gritted his teeth. This can't happen, he told himself again, grimly. I'm not going to let it happen.

Jeffrey thumbed through the address book. He was going to call Rebecca, tell her he had to work tomorrow, and that was that. He certainly wasn't going to volunteer to go over there another time. Of course, if Rebecca suggested it . . . oh, well. Never mind.

Where was Rebecca's phone number, anyway? Then Jeffrey remembered that Rebecca had never given him her phone number. He recalled that she'd shocked him by explaining that she liked living alone with nothing to disturb her.

Rebecca didn't have a telephone.

Chapter 18

Later that same evening, Mr. Smeal stood by the screen door and looked outside. He was looking forward to the sunset. He thought it was the perfect time of day. It was so peaceful when the tender pink light breathed across the sky.

Mr. Smeal pushed the screen door open and let it slam as he stepped out onto the back porch. Immediately, a wall of heat hit him in the face. Stubbornly, Mr. Smeal refused to let it stop him from sitting in his favorite chair.

Stepping down off the porch and into the yard, Mr. Smeal sat down in a lawn chair that he'd placed under a tree. With sweat rolling off his brow, he gazed around the quiet yard.

This time tomorrow I'll be headed toward another moving job instead of relaxing, he thought, looking up at the sky. Well, at least most of the job would be done in the cooler part of the evening instead of the sweltering heat. Jeffrey should be glad the job was late in the day instead of trying to get out of it.

Young people today, thought Mr. Smeal. They want everything to be easy. He sighed. He knew he wasn't really being fair. Jeffrey was a good young man. He would go far. Jeffrey's right, too, he said to himself. I shouldn't get so excited. He sighed again. There was nothing he could do about it.

Suddenly, Mr. Smeal felt an uneasy chill pass through his body. It was the sort of feeling you have when someone is watching you. He looked up and saw a dark bird perched in a nearby tree. It was an unusual bird. Extraordinary, really. It was so beautiful. Its ebony feathers gleamed, reflecting the sun so that the bird glowed.

Mr. Smeal tried to decide what sort of bird it was. A raven, perhaps. What was a raven doing in his backyard? He'd never seen one there before.

As Mr. Smeal stared, he almost thought he saw the bird changing before his eyes. It was getting bigger. He looked away for a moment and blinked rapidly. When he looked back at the bird, he thought that his eyesight was failing him. Or perhaps there was some trick of the light. The bird had gotten bigger still.

Mr. Smeal fidgeted in his chair. He decided he didn't like the look of that bird. It made him uncomfortable. Something about its eyes . . . they actually looked *red*.

Mr. Smeal got to his feet. He didn't want to sit there in the yard any longer. As he got up he could feel the bird's eyes on him. When he looked at the bird again, it actually seemed to be staring at him *reproachfully*.

As he walked out of the yard, Mr. Smeal was embarrassed for feeling nervous. His breathing had quickened, and he tried to slow it down. It was only a bird. What's the matter with you, he chided himself. Are you starting to go soft in the head?

As soon as he felt the sidewalk under his feet, Mr. Smeal started to feel better. He walked to the front of his house and toward the end of the block. See? He said to himself. It's just another evening.

Then he looked up, and saw the bird flying above him in the sky . . . following him.

Mr. Smeal tried to ignore the bird. He fought to keep his pace unhurried and leisurely. But each time he looked up the bird was overhead, flying in slow, lazy circles in the sky.

His feet began moving faster and faster, as if beyond the control of his mind. The bird continued to circle overhead.

In moments, Mr. Smeal dropped all pretense of being unafraid and gave himself over completely to panic. He ran. The bird continued to follow. Mr. Smeal ran faster. He ran harder than he had in years.

The bird kept circling overhead.

With his heart hammering, Mr. Smeal kept running. His breath came in hard, desperate gasps. His chest heaved. Sweat poured from him, running down his forehead and stinging into his eyes. Somehow, he kept on moving, his legs pumping frantically. He had lost all sense of reason.

Gulping air, Mr. Smeal looked up, knowing in advance that the bird would be there. It was. But it wasn't circling anymore. The bird was flying in a straight line above him, staring down at him with hard, angry, eyes.

Something was going to happen. Paralyzed with fear, Mr. Smeal stood still and raised his hands to shield his face. The bird dropped from the sky like a stone.

Mr. Smeal felt a soft rush of wind from the bird's wings. Its feathers brushed his face.

Time seemed to stand still. And then Mr. Smeal felt the first razor-sharp slash as the bird ripped into the flesh of his arm. He screamed as the bird slashed again, piercing through his shirt and the skin on his back.

The bird attacked him with its pointed beak, and Mr. Smeal felt blood running down his face. The talons cut into him again and again. He screamed, louder this time. But no one heard him.

Then, mercifully, a velvet darkness enveloped him as he lost consciousness.

Chapter 19

Jeffrey sat on the living room sofa, leaning forward, his arms resting on his knees. He was thinking about Rebecca.

Without a telephone in her house, the only way to contact her was by driving out to where she lived. He decided that was the only thing to do. He couldn't just fail to show up tomorrow.

The problem was that Jeffrey had plans with Barbara. He had promised to take her to the Schooner Inn, a new restaurant out by the shore she'd been talking about.

It took an hour to get to the restaurant, and an hour to drive to Rebecca's house. Jeffrey looked at his watch. It was nearly seven o'clock. He was supposed to pick Barbara up at seven-thirty. Well — they'd just have to go to dinner a little later. Barbara would understand.

Jeffrey got up and walked to the window. Then he came back to the sofa and sat down again. He knew that as soon as he had found out about the moving job tomorrow evening, he should have told Rebecca that he wouldn't be able to pose for her. *But he hadn't.*

In his heart he knew it was because he wanted to see her. He hadn't wanted to tell her he wouldn't be there. Secretly, he'd been hoping to find some way to be with her after all. He hadn't wanted to admit it to himself. But it was true.

Jeffrey got up and walked into the dining room. It occurred to him that he could pick Barbara up and take her with him to Rebecca's house, and then they could go to dinner from there. *Barbara would understand.*

He felt a pang of guilt because he knew that Barbara wouldn't object. What made him feel guiltier was that he knew in his heart that he didn't want to take Barbara with him to Rebecca's. He wanted to see Rebecca alone.

Jeffrey was standing in the same spot in the dining room, his hands in his back pockets, when his mother came into the house. "Jeffrey, you look lost in thought," she remarked. "Is something on your mind?"

Jeffrey tried to shake off the troubling

thoughts. "Oh, no, not really. I was just thinking, that's all."

The phone rang. "I'll get it," Mrs. Thomas said, going into the kitchen. In a moment she walked back into the dining room. "It's for you, Jeffrey." She looked slightly puzzled. "It's Mr. Smeal's sister. Something's happened."

Jeffrey went into the kitchen and picked up the phone. "This is Jeffrey Thomas."

The voice on the other end of the line was firm and sharp in tone — a female version of Mr. Smeal's voice. "Jeffrey, I know you've been working for my brother and — well — there won't be any more work this summer. My brother's had an accident."

"What happened?" Jeffrey asked, concerned.

For a moment there was silence. When the woman spoke, her voice was slightly shaky. "Has my brother been acting different lately? Have you noticed anything strange about him?"

Jeffrey felt a prickling sensation ripple through his body like a wave. "He's an excitable man. But there's nothing new about that. He works too hard, but there's nothing new about that, either."

"Oh, my."

The woman's voice was shakier now, as if

she was controlling herself with a considerable effort.

"Maybe my brother needs a rest. I hope that's all. I just don't know. I just don't know."

"Take it easy," Jeffrey said gently. "Tell me what happened."

Jeffrey heard a deep sigh. "My brother called me up tonight, babbling almost incoherently. I finally understood that he was talking about being attacked by some strange bird. He said the bird had followed him, intending to attack him. Then the bird had slashed and bitten him. He told me to come right over and take him to the hospital." The woman started to cry.

"That's horrible," Jeffrey said. "The poor man." He told the woman to calm down. "Perhaps it's not as bad as it seems. What did they say at the hospital?"

The woman continued to sob for a moment. Then she recovered. "I didn't take my brother to the hospital yet," she said, her voice steady. "I'm afraid he'll have to go there soon, though I'm not sure what kind of treatment he needs. You see, my brother is convinced that the bird attacked him, and now he's slashed and bleeding." There was a pause before she continued. "My brother hasn't got a scratch on him."

A few moments later the conversation

ended. Jeffrey hung up the phone, a queasy feeling in his stomach. He was stunned by the news about Mr. Smeal. Whatever the man was, Jeffrey certainly never felt that Mr. Smeal was mentally unstable. To think that he had simply cracked all of a sudden was impossible.

Had there been something wrong with Mr. Smeal that Jeffrey had simply failed to see?

As disturbing as any of his other thoughts was the fact that through all of them, Jeffrey kept thinking one thing. Now nothing would keep him from being with Rebecca tomorrow.

Chapter 20

"This place is wonderful." Barbara reached across the table and gave Jeffrey's hand a squeeze. Jeffrey agreed with her. The Schooner Inn was a terrific place.

The restaurant was built on the water. Part of it actually projected out over the waves. Jeffrey and Barbara had an excellent table by the window, overlooking the sea. Occasionally the surf could be heard through the strains of soft music in the restaurant.

Jeffrey wished he could share Barbara's enthusiasm, but he felt too distracted. He looked across the table. Barbara was smiling at him. In the soft light from the candles on the table, her eyes sparkled.

Jeffrey looked away. He had a vision of Rebecca, standing in an empty room, her face lit up by a hundred candle flames. The fire was reflected in her smouldering violet eyes, and her soft red lips . . .

"Jeffrey."

Dimly, Jeffrey heard Barbara's voice.

"Jeffrey, you're a million miles away tonight."

Jeffrey snapped back to reality. "Sorry, Barbara. I guess I'm worried about Mr. Smeal."

Barbara nodded sympathetically.

You're so kind and good, Jeffrey thought, gazing at her. Barbara was always there for him. Throughout all the years that he had known her, Barbara had never done a single petty or mean-spirited thing. And he would need many more than two hands to count the friends who had turned to Barbara when they needed someone to talk to. Hers was the truest heart he had ever known.

But Jeffrey couldn't deny that something about his feelings for her had changed, much as he hated to admit it. He still loved her, but when he looked at her he didn't feel as complete as he once had.

Her appearance was unsettling. Jeffrey missed her red-gold curls — not that that was what made the difference in his feelings. But she didn't look like the same Barbara. And she always wore black now. It didn't suit her the way it did Rebecca. Perhaps that was the problem. Every time he saw Barbara dressed in black, he was reminded of Rebecca.

"Jeffrey, you're far away again," Barbara said. "You were saying that you're worried about Mr. Smeal. That's the strangest story about him imagining he was attacked by a bird. It's so sad."

"Yeah, it's pretty terrible. I hope they can help him. Unfortunately, it means that I'm out of a job right now. Dad said he'd take me on at the hardware store, but there's no point in that. He's had old Sammy working there for years, and he doesn't need any more help."

"It's too bad," Barbara said, looking concerned. "It's not a good time to find a job now, either. Everyone's already got their summer jobs." She tilted her head thoughtfully.

"I know!" Barbara brightened suddenly. "The other day Rebecca said . . ."

"Rebecca, Rebecca, Rebecca!" Jeffrey shouted. He threw his napkin on the table. "Why do we always have to talk about *her?* I'm out with *you!*"

Barbara drew back, stung by the anger in his words. Her eyes began to fill with tears. People at the tables around them stopped talking and stared. They were surrounded by an uncomfortable silence.

Jeffrey was shocked at his own outburst. It

had just happened so suddenly. Something had seized him inside and he'd hardly known what he was doing.

"Barbara, oh, Barbara. I'm so sorry." Jeffrey reached across the table and stroked her cheek, too overcome with remorse to care that others in the restaurant were staring at them. Barbara sat stiffly, looking at her plate, her shoulders hunched and her hands in her lap.

A man who was wandering through the restaurant selling roses passed by their table. Jeffrey motioned him over, selected a rose, and gave the man some bills.

"Barbara," Jeffrey said, placing the rose in front of her. "I love you and I'm terribly sorry. I'm just tense, that's all. Please forgive me."

Barbara looked up slowly and dabbed at her eyes. She looked at Jeffrey's earnest face. "Don't ever snap at me like that again," she said. Then she smiled at him and picked up the rose.

People at the nearby tables started talking again. They smiled to themselves. A lover's quarrel . . . now ended.

"What I was trying to tell you, Jeffrey," Barbara said as they resumed their conversation, "was that Rebecca mentioned needing to hire someone to do some work around her place. She said she needs landscaping and some things fixed and — oh, lots of things. She might as well hire you as anybody, right?"

Jeffrey looked into Barbara's eyes, overcome with affection for her. How many other girls would suggest that their boyfriends spend time with Rebecca? Not many, thought Jeffrey. But Barbara didn't have a jealous bone in her body.

"I don't know if I want to do that kind of work," Jeffrey said doubtfully. "And she probably couldn't pay me much."

"That's not true, Jeffrey," Barbara protested. "She says her parents gave her a lot of money to fix the place up. I think they're rich. You ought to at least ask Rebecca about the job."

Jeffrey touched Barbara's hand. "All right."

Later that night Jeffrey held Barbara close and kissed her tenderly. There was no one in his heart but her.

The next morning, however, Jeffrey woke with his head filled anew with thoughts of Rebecca. He had slept badly and felt out of step all day long. He would put something down and then forget where it was, and grumble as he looked for it. Again and again he looked at his watch and thought of the time he would see Rebecca.

But as it happened, Rebecca cancelled their date. She did it without phoning or talking to Jeffrey.

Jeffrey didn't know that Rebecca wouldn't be seeing him that night until he went out to his car to drive to her house. There was a note taped to his windshield. *Jeffrey, you can't come over tonight. Something has come up*, was all it said.

Angry and disappointed, and disturbed that he was either of those things, Jeffrey crumpled the note and threw it on the ground. He had been home all day, and Rebecca had put the note on his windshield without even bothering to ring the doorbell.

Well, fine, Jeffrey said to himself. Now he didn't have to bother sitting there while Rebecca painted. As far as he was concerned, he didn't owe her a favor anymore. When he saw her he'd tell her, too. Jeffrey stormed into the house.

But as day after day went by with no sign of Rebecca, Jeffrey grew more and more restless and absentminded. He tossed and turned all night and woke up tired and haggard.

He snapped at Barbara and his brother

Tony. When his mother asked him to pick up her car from the mechanic, Jeffrey arrived too late and they were closed. He forgot to make another cash deposit for his father, who was annoyed with him for days.

Jeffrey asked himself again and again, where had Rebecca gone? He drove around the town hoping for a glimpse of her. When he was talking to his friends at Sharkey's, his attention wandered as his eyes searched for her. Hardest of all was the time he spent with Barbara — wishing she was Rebecca.

Finally, filled with humiliation, he drove to Rebecca's house. He felt a sense of total dejection when the house greeted him with emptiness.

By the time a week and a half had gone by and Rebecca had still not appeared, people were beginning to wonder what was happening to Jeffrey. He certainly wasn't himself.

Chapter 21

It was almost two weeks since anyone had seen Rebecca, and then, suddenly, she reappeared. She came roaring into town in her red convertible just as she had on that first day.

While she had been gone, there had been a break in the heat. Now it reappeared, more punishing than ever. This time it continued into the night. There was no drop in temperature, and no fog rolled in. Just heat . . . day and night.

Jeffrey was short-tempered and listless. He stayed in bed until nearly noon. At night he slept fitfully, tossing and turning. His sleep was full of dreams of Rebecca. They were dreams that he longed for, yet at the same time they terrified him. He would lie awake long after he'd gone to bed. Then he would pray for sleep, for the chance to be with Rebecca, even in a dream.

Jeffrey thought he would never see Rebecca again. And then one day, she pulled her car up next to him as he was leaving Abbott's grocery. "Hi, Jeffrey," she said, as if she had never been away at all.

Stunned, Jeffrey stared at her for several moments before he could speak. He had thought of her constantly while she was gone. Though many times he had tried to put her out of his mind, her absence had only intensified his longing.

In his mind's eye, Jeffrey had recreated the glow of her ivory skin, the luminous shimmer of her hair, the graceful curves of her body, the haunting light in her violet eyes. He had conjured up vision after vision of her, all so vivid he could almost touch her. And yet now that she was here it was as if he had only recalled a pale fraction of the beauty that overwhelmed his eyes and filled his heart.

Jeffrey had planned to be pleasant, if he ever saw Rebecca again. Pleasant, but cool. Now he could only stare at her and breathe, "Where have you been?"

Rebecca threw back her head and laughed, filling the air with silvery music. "Oh, here and there, doing this and that. Nothing important. I just had to get away and be alone, that's all. You want to be alone, sometimes, don't you?"

"Of course," Jeffrey replied. "I understand." To himself he thought, grimly, that being alone was not exactly what he'd had in mind lately.

"Get in, and we can go for a ride," Rebecca said, the light dancing in her violet eyes.

"Sure," Jeffrey said, trying to sound casual. "I'm in no hurry." His mouth was dry as he opened the car door and got inside.

As she drove, Rebecca's hair streamed out behind her in an ebony plume. She wore a sleeveless black top made of a stretchy, clinging material that molded to the curve of her body. Black denim shorts revealed her long, slender legs.

"I ran into Barbara earlier. She says you're out of a job, Jeffrey." Rebecca's tapered fingers turned the steering wheel, easing the car out onto the highway. Her red nails shone like rubies.

"That's right," Jeffrey replied, forcing himself not to look at Rebecca too long.

"Well, as Barbara said she mentioned to you, I'm looking for someone to do some work around the place." Rebecca glanced at Jeffrey from under long lashes.

"Barbara said something about it." Jeffrey tried to get control of the feelings that were whirling around in his heart. He felt strangely off-balance, as if he might fall, even though he was sitting down.

"So, are you . . . interested?" Rebecca turned to look at him directly, her eyes locking with his for a long moment.

"Definitely," Jeffrey said, without hesitation.

"Well, then," Rebecca said, her voice lilting softly now, "I want to get started right away."

The following afternoon, Jeffrey started working at Rebecca's. She didn't want him to arrive too early, which puzzled him. But he didn't ask why.

As Jeffrey drove to Rebecca's, he pondered the fact that there were all kinds of problems in his life now. Nothing went smoothly, not even little things. He forgot things, lost things, stores were closed when he arrived, or out of what he had come to buy. It was silly, but it was beginning to seem almost like part of a plan.

Like today. Later that evening he was going to a party that Barbara's parents were having at the country club to celebrate their older daughter's college graduation. They wanted it to be formal, so he'd have to wear a tuxedo.

Naturally, the tuxedo wasn't ready when Jeffrey had gone to pick it up. The way things had been going, he wasn't even surprised.

Now Barbara would have to pick up the tuxedo and meet him at Rebecca's. He'd have to clean up and change at Rebecca's, and then follow Barbara to the country club.

Jeffrey reached Rebecca's house and was stunned as always by the bleak, desolate appearance of the place. It looked deserted. The idea that anyone was living there was preposterous.

Jeffrey parked the car and went up on the porch. The front door was open just a little. He pushed it open a bit farther and called, "Rebecca? Rebecca, are you there?"

Silence settled thickly around him.

"Rebecca?" Jeffrey called again. He waited, listening.

After a few more moments had gone by, Jeffrey pushed back the door and stepped into the house. He drew himself up sharply as he looked around the room.

Streams of light fought their way through windows clouded with the dirt of years gone by. A heavy coating of dust lay over everything, painting it with a coat of gray fuzz.

As Jeffrey stepped into the room, his shoes

left sharp footprints in the dust. The corners of the room were so filled with cobwebs they looked as if they were heavy with Spanish moss. Cobwebs hung from the ceiling. Jeffrey expected spiders to suddenly plummet and land on him.

There certainly is a lot of work to be done here, Jeffrey thought, his scalp prickling. *Too much work.* He glanced at the staircase. Could it be that Rebecca lived on the second floor, and was fixing the place from the top down?

Jeffrey walked over and leaned on the banister. Immediately, he drew back his hands. His fingers and palms were smeared with sooty dust and dirt where he had touched the railing. Grimacing with distaste, he wiped his hands on his jeans.

There were holes in several of the steps. The staircase didn't look very sturdy or safe. He couldn't imagine Rebecca walking up and down it.

Jeffrey's heart thudded hollowly in his chest. Some of the windows were still boarded up. Rough-hewn planks were nailed across them every which way.

This place is ghastly, he thought.

Just as he was about to go outside, Jeffrey felt a light, refreshing breeze waft through the house. Where could it have come from? he wondered.

The breeze blew over him again, soft and cool. And then he heard, clear and unmistakable, the breeze call his name.

Jeffrey. Jeffrey.

Chapter 22

"Jeffrey," the soft, haunting voice whispered again. Then Jeffrey saw Rebecca standing before him, appearing suddenly as if out of the air.

Jeffrey stared at her, his face lit with wonder. Her image filled his eyes, his heart, his soul, with enchantment. So overwhelmed was Jeffrey with the sheer presence of Rebecca, the glowing, vibrance of her, that the room fell away and he saw only her.

"Jeffrey," Rebecca said again in a crystal whisper that reached through the haze that clouded his mind. Slowly, Jeffrey began to emerge from his trance. Gradually, the room came back into focus. Once again he saw the dust around his feet and the dirt on the windows.

"Rebecca," Jeffrey said slowly, caressing

her name. "I didn't hear you come in. I was looking at the house."

"Yes." The smoky sunlight in the room lit up Rebecca's face. "As you can see, it needs a lot of work. But I'd like you to start working outside."

With an imperious wave of her hand, she led the way onto the porch, motioning for Jeffrey to follow her.

Outside, Jeffrey took several deep breaths. The fresh air cleared his mind a little.

Moving ahead, Rebecca walked down the path that led through the yard. Jeffrey followed. Midway down the path, Rebecca stood still.

"The first thing we have to do is to get things growing around here again," Rebecca said, turning to Jeffrey. She flashed him a dazzling smile that told him there was no question in her mind that he could accomplish whatever she asked.

Jeffrey, however, concentrated on keeping his face from revealing his own doubts. He had never seen such parched, lifeless earth.

Shading his eyes from the sun, Jeffrey surveyed the landscape surrounding Rebecca's house. The strangeness of the scene caused a dull buzz of alarm in his brain.

As he looked into the distance, Jeffrey could

see the trees, wilting but still green. He could see the ground a short way away covered with a tangled riot of weeds and grasses. But about twenty yards or so from Rebecca's house, all growth stopped abruptly, as if the earth had been scorched.

Jeffrey looked back at Rebecca, her beauty blazing in front of him. "The soil needs nourishment," he told her. "It looks like all the life has been sucked out of it. Before I can do anything, we should drive to the nursery and get some supplies."

"Drive to the nursery," echoed Rebecca, her face rigidly calm. "No, I don't feel like driving to the nursery," she said quickly, in a tone that invited no further discussion. "What we need to do now is to have a discussion and come up with a plan for getting things done around here. Let's sit on the porch and talk."

Without waiting for Jeffrey to respond, Rebecca started walking. Jeffrey walked along by her side. "I hope you'll be available every day," Rebecca said, gazing up at Jeffrey as she sat down on the porch steps. Jeffrey marvelled that anyone could perform such an ordinary act as sitting down, with such extraordinary grace. He sat down beside her, and they began to talk.

Jeffrey didn't know when, or how it happened, but the topic of work was discarded almost immediately in favor of more personal conversation. Soon, Jeffrey found himself discussing his hopes and dreams, and even his fears . . . and feeling that no one he had ever spoken to had understood him quite so well before.

Barbara Matthew decided to take one last look in the mirror before driving to Rebecca's house. She liked what she saw, thinking that the sleeveless black dress that skimmed her knees gave her just the right touch of glamour and sophistication.

Fortunately, sweet, gentle Barbara was blind to the vision others would see when they looked at her. They would have a vision of a girl who was overwhelmed by the blackness of the dress. They would feel there was something jarring and unsettling about Barbara's appearance. The humidity had made her hair curl too tightly. It was beginning to look like orange fuzz.

Smiling, and full of expectation about the evening ahead, Barbara hurried out the door to her car. Jeffrey's tuxedo was already hanging in the back, encased in black plastic. Barbara glanced at it lovingly, thinking how handsome Jeffrey would look wearing it. Then she started driving to Rebecca's.

It was early evening, but the sun still blazed like an angry fireball in the sky. Barbara was full of eager anticipation as she drove along the road that led up to the cliffs. Out the car window she could see the sun sparkling like diamonds on the ocean.

Then, suddenly, swiftly, the sky turned an ominous shade of gray. The sea, which a moment before had glittered with jewels of golden sunlight, was steely and dark. It was like seeing someone's friendly smile explode in an outburst of rage in an instant.

Barbara felt her flesh tingle, but not from any coolness in the air. The heat continued, even more oppressive than before. Her skin was prickling with wariness. What was happening all around her was eerily frightening.

Then, painting an even more vivid picture of unreality, the sky grew darker, and heavy mists began to rise from the ground as if the earth was exhaling clouds of steam. The mists swirled around Barbara's car, becoming thicker and thicker until she could no longer see where she was going. Barbara felt danger looming ahead. The mist whispered to her silently of unnamed terrors lurking in it, unseen. The mists became the claws of some monster that wanted to fasten them around her throat.

Far below her, Barbara could hear the ocean pounding angrily on the rocks, a hard, threatening sound — as if the waves were trying to leap up onto the land. Then they would unleash their fury and attack some unsuspecting victim, and rip the poor creature's heart out.

Her panic building with each passing moment, Barbara pulled over to the side of the road, afraid she would drive the car into the sea. There she sat, imagining monsters lurking in the mists, waiting to pounce on her. Fear played on her mind until she almost believed she was going crazy, and there really were whispering voices all around her.

Barbara's only comfort was in thinking of Jeffrey. She was sure that as soon as she didn't arrive at Rebecca's on time, Jeffrey would start looking for her.

Chapter 23

The light on Rebecca's face was no longer full of fire, but softer and mellower. It made Jeffrey look around, suddenly aware of his surroundings as he had not been since beginning the conversation with Rebecca. Startled, he saw that the sun was low on the horizon, a peach-orange ball breathing the first glint of evening across the sky.

"Where has the time gone?" Jeffrey said in amazement. Hurriedly, he looked at his watch. "It's eight o'clock!" he exclaimed, leaping to his feet. He peered anxiously down the dirt road that led from the main road to Rebecca's house. "Barbara is awfully late," he said, his brows knitted together.

Rebecca crossed her legs languidly. "She'll be along soon," she said, rocking one foot slowly back and forth. "She probably took a long time getting dressed. This is a formal affair, isn't it? She must want to look perfect."

Jeffrey shook his head slowly. "No. Barbara has never been late before." His jaw tightened and he looked thoughtful. "I should have been watching for her. I shouldn't have lost track of the time."

Rebecca looked at Jeffrey for a moment, her violet eyes deep and mysterious. Slowly, she got to her feet. Pressing her ruby lips together she looked as if she were thinking over what to do.

"We've got to go and look for Barbara right now," Jeffrey said, firmly. "Let's go."

When Jeffrey used that tone, people did what he said. But as Jeffrey took a step toward the red convertible, Rebecca didn't make a move. She pulled a black ribbon from the back pocket of her jeans and began tying back her mass of black hair.

"If you're driving around looking for Barbara, you'll miss her if she comes *here*." Rebecca's ruby lips curved in a smile.

"She'll wait, then. She'll know I've gone looking when she didn't arrive on time. I'm sure something has happened."

Rebecca nodded, her expression unreadable. "All right. We'll look for Barbara."

As they drove along, the twilight deepened into darkness, and there was no sign of Barbara's car. Jeffrey called her house from a roadside phone, but there was no answer. Sighing with frustration, Jeffrey left a message on the answering machine, and got back in the car.

It was a warm, clear night. Jeffrey looked at the twinkling stars in the sky, and was miserable. Something might have happened to Barbara, and when he should have been thinking of her, thoughts of someone else had filled his mind and heart. He clenched his fists in his lap.

The soft night air blew against their faces. The temperature was lower than it had been all summer long. It was a lovely night for a drive, but Jeffrey had not the least bit of enjoyment in it. He ached to find Barbara.

Rebecca, however, sat behind the wheel looking quite relaxed. "You worry too much," she said, her voice slightly tinged with amusement. "You'll make yourself sick. Why don't you talk about something to give your mind a rest?"

When Jeffrey said nothing, a flicker of annoyance crossed Rebecca's beautiful face.

"We ought to go back and see if Barbara is

waiting at your house," Jeffrey said, finally.

Without a word, Rebecca turned the car around at the first opportunity. The two of them started back to her house in silence.

When they had driven for a while, Rebecca began tapping her red fingernails in a staccato against the steering wheel. "Honestly," she said, her crystal voice edged with brittleness, "you haven't seen a car accident. I'm sure Barbara is perfectly all right."

Jeffrey sat mutely. After a moment Rebecca sighed, almost inaudibly, and drove on. Then they saw something up ahead, by the side of the road.

"It's Barbara's car!" Jeffrey said, astonished. "We passed this exact spot before." He looked at Rebecca, who shrugged noncommittally.

Rebecca pulled her red convertible behind Barbara's cream-colored Volvo. As soon as Barbara saw Jeffrey, she bolted from her car and ran toward him. He went to meet her.

"Jeffrey!" Barbara wrapped her arms around his neck. Tears were streaming down her cheeks. "I was so frightened. Everything was so *strange*."

Rebecca sat still, making no move to leave the convertible. She stared straight ahead,

her eyes smouldering, as Jeffrey and Barbara talked.

Her arm around Jeffrey's waist, Barbara turned to Rebecca. "I'm so glad to see you!"

A breathtaking smile transformed Rebecca's face. "I'm glad to see you, too, Barbara. I was concerned when we couldn't find you."

"Tell us what happened," Jeffrey said urgently.

Barbara was wide-eyed. "I was driving to pick you up, Jeffrey, and it got so dark. It happened so suddenly, I felt . . ." Barbara's voice trailed off. She twisted her hands.

"Go on," Jeffrey said, softly. He stroked her shoulder.

Barbara sighed. "When I couldn't see to drive anymore, I got so scared that I pulled the car over to the side of the road. I was afraid that I hadn't pulled over far enough, and someone else who was driving along and couldn't see might hit me." Her lips trembled. "I didn't want to hit the cliffs, either."

"Wait. I don't understand." Jeffrey took Barbara's face in his hands and looked into her eyes. "Why couldn't you see, Barbara? Why not?"

Barbara's eyes widened even more. "Why, Jeffrey — you know, don't you? It was the mist. It came out of nowhere . . . so thick . . ."

Stunned, Jeffrey looked at Barbara.

Finally, it was Rebecca who spoke up, in her lilting voice. "Why, Barbara, you can't be serious. The air was clear tonight — clearer than it's been in a long time."

Chapter 24

No matter how impossible Jeffrey and Rebecca told her it was, Barbara stuck to her story that her car had been enveloped in mist. And although there had been no fog at night for over two weeks, later that night the fog came back, almost as if mocking Jeffrey for disbelieving Barbara's story.

The fog drifted inland from some place far out at sea. It blanketed Winthrop at the exact moment that it invaded Jeffrey's dreams, some time just before midnight.

Tossing and turning, sweating in spite of the air-conditioned coolness of his room, Jeffrey rolled this way and that across the bed. His movements were twisted and frantic, as if he was trying desperately to get away from something.

But Jeffrey's mind, drifting in the velvet curtain of a dream, was doing something very different. In his mind, Jeffrey was following someone, seeking the person as if seeking the truth.

Jeffrey was deep in the woods, moving through leafless trees in the night. The full moon was high in the sky, its light bathing the ground through the bare branches.

Jeffrey couldn't hear his footsteps on the ground, couldn't feel the branches brushing against him as he moved. But he could hear and feel the blood surging through his veins. He could feel the steady *beat, beat, beat* of his heart.

All of Jeffrey's energy was focused on following . . . what? At first he did not know. He only knew that he *must* follow.

When he saw the shadow through the trees, he knew he was getting closer. He walked faster, his feet feeling heavy and clumsy.

Gradually, he could see that he was following a young woman dressed all in black. Her cloak billowed out before him, dark and silken. He thought he could reach out and touch it. But when he stretched out his hand, he discovered that his eyes had deceived him. It was still very far away.

Jeffrey hurried on, his heart pumping harder

now, the blood surging through his veins. The shadow ahead called to him. *"Jeffrey."* At each sound of her voice, fires flamed up inside him.

Wait. Jeffrey tried to call out to her. His lips formed the word, but his mouth was too dry and he was much too breathless to say it.

"Jeffrey," the shadow called again, and Jeffrey stumbled on. He was gasping for air now, his heart pounding hard and painfully in his chest. Still, desperately, he kept on following.

Then when Jeffrey had exhausted every bit of strength, all of his reserves, every last particle of willpower he possessed, the shadowy figure turned toward him.

Her alabaster skin glowed in the moonlight. Her dark hair and filmy black cloak gave her the look of a creature made of the night. Most remarkable were her eyes that looked at him and saw his soul.

Hypnotized, Jeffrey couldn't look away from her. She swayed before his eyes, floating above the ground as she moved toward him, her hands outstretched. Jeffrey yearned for her, longed to go to her, but he could not move.

Now he knew he was looking at Rebecca.

Rebecca moved toward Jeffrey, nearer and nearer, until her hand was on the side of his face. Her touch was electric.

In a trance, Jeffrey remained motionless as Rebecca's face drew closer and closer to his. He closed his eyes, and felt the softness of her lips, burning with passion.

Jeffrey's entire body was on fire. He drew Rebecca into his arms, kissing her deeply.

For an instant, Jeffrey was bathed in rapture. And then he felt something inside of him break with a white-hot flash of searing pain. He saw himself falling, falling away from Rebecca into darkness. As he fell into the pit he reached out to Rebecca, convulsed with terror. And she smiled at him.

As if outside his body, Jeffrey could see himself falling, his arms outstretched, his face contorted in agony. Then, suddenly, he landed.

He was enveloped in velvet darkness. From somewhere far away he could hear music, and the sound of someone sobbing with heartrending grief.

Jeffrey looked down at himself. Why was his face so still, and his complexion so strange, as if it was made of wax?

Then his heart lurched. He wanted to scream, to run, but he couldn't move or make a sound. He knew he never would again. For this was Jeffrey's funeral.

He was looking at himself in his coffin.

Chapter 25

One week after Jeffrey's first dream of Rebecca, he and Paul sat in a coffee shop next to Stanton's jewelry store in Winthrop. Outside the window, a gray fog hung over the town. For the past few days, it had blanketed everything, spoiling with its atmosphere of gloom the enjoyment people felt at the break in the heat.

"The hamburgers here aren't as good as Sharkey's," Paul said, crumpling his napkin and throwing it on a plate.

"No way," Jeffrey agreed.

Paul leaned forward, his face serious. "I have to tell you something, Jeffrey. You look terrible lately. Is something wrong?"

Jeffrey raked his hand through his hair. "It's hard to explain. I've never felt this way — like things are coming unraveled. Maybe it's just because I haven't slept well for a while now.

I have these dreams — nightmares really. In them . . . I'm running through the woods at night, that's all I remember. Except that every time, at the end, I see myself in a coffin — and then I wake up, and for a while I'm terrified."

Paul regarded Jeffrey in silence. He wanted to say something that would help, but he didn't have a clue as to what it should be. He had never seen his friend look so haggard.

Jeffrey's skin had a peculiar grayish cast underneath his tan. His eyes had dark circles under them, and he'd lost weight. He looked like someone haunted by some secret fear.

Jeffrey saw the concern on Paul's face. "Don't worry, Paul. I'll be fine as soon as my sleep straightens out."

"Yeah, that's right," Paul agreed, wishing he was sure of his words.

"Come on, let's get over to Stanton's. I've got to get Barbara's birthday present. I want to buy her something really nice. I've got some things to make up to her."

"Like? . . ." Paul invited explanation.

Jeffrey clasped his hands on the table. "Like ruining her sister's graduation party for her, for one thing. She was late and I should have gone looking for her, but I was talking to Rebecca. When we finally found her where she'd pulled off the road, she was crazy with fear, and told me some wild story I can't even figure out yet. And by the time we got to the party, her father was really worried. He was furious with me when he heard what had happened."

Paul looked at Jeffrey quizzically. "Why was he mad at *you?*"

"Because Barbara had pulled off the highway not far from Rebecca's house. It shouldn't have taken long to find her. But I didn't start looking until she'd been over an hour late."

Paul nodded. "Yeah, why *did* you wait so long?"

Jeffrey shook his head. "It's really strange. While I was talking to Rebecca, the time just flew by. I had no idea it was so late, I really didn't." Jeffrey looked thoughtful. "The other weird thing is that we should've seen Barbara's car right away. But I'm sure we passed by the spot, and she wasn't there — yet when we went by it again, she was. I don't see how she could have gotten there without passing us."

"Let's go," Paul said after a moment. He couldn't comment on Jeffrey's story. He simply had no idea what to say. He'd never heard Jeffrey talk like this. One thing stood out in his mind. The way Jeffrey looked when he said Rebecca's name.

They paid the check and went next door to

Stanton's jewelry store. Stanton's had been in Winthrop for fifty years. Jeffrey's father and Martin Stanton, son of the founder and the current owner, had been childhood friends. Mr. Stanton waved to Jeffrey as he walked in the door.

"Hey, Jeffrey, how's the family?"

"Fine, thanks," Jeffrey told him. He could see Mr. Stanton eyeing him. He's thinking I look awful, Jeffrey knew. "Mr. Stanton, this is my friend, Paul Davis."

"Pleased to meet you, Paul." Mr. Stanton and Paul shook hands.

While Jeffrey and Mr. Stanton chatted briefly, Paul took in the interior of Stanton's jewelry store. The large, high-ceilinged room had rows of glass cases filled with glittering jewels. This was a place for *serious* jewelry, there was nothing funky about it. If Jeffrey was buying Barbara's present here, then he must be serious, too, Paul thought. Still, the look that had passed over Jeffrey's face when he mentioned Rebecca haunted him.

"We're going to look at some necklaces," Jeffrey told Paul. Mr. Stanton led them to a glass case at the front of the store.

"Steve will help you, Jeffrey," Mr. Stanton said before he walked away, gesturing to a young man behind the counter.

Half an hour later, Jeffrey was still looking at velvet-lined boxes full of necklaces. Again and again, he had picked up the same one, a gold heart with a diamond chip on a delicate gold chain. "Barbara would love this," Jeffrey said, admiring it.

"But you said it's too expensive about five times, Jeffrey. What's it going to be? Either you decide you've got the money after all, or you decide on something else." Paul was struck by Jeffrey's indecisiveness — something else he'd never seen in him before.

Jeffrey put the necklace down, then picked it up again. He was gazing at it when Paul noticed a hush fall over the store. When he saw who had entered, he knew why. It was Rebecca.

Rebecca was striking in a high-necked, sleeveless black dress with a hem that fell several inches above her knees. She wore her black hair loose, tumbling over her shoulders, its silken length gleaming. As always, she was so vibrant and alive that she stood apart from others. She came toward Paul and Jeffrey.

"Hi, Rebecca. You look great, as always," Paul said. Jeffrey looked up from the necklace, startled. "Rebecca," he said. Paul saw the same look he had seen earlier, a kind of long-

ing, a yearning, in Jeffrey's eyes. It made Paul
uncomfortable.

"How lovely," Rebecca said, looking at the
boxes of necklaces on the counter. "Barbara
will be so pleased with her birthday present,"
she said in her silvery voice. Paul noticed that
everyone in the store was staring at Rebecca,
but she paid no attention, nor acted the least
bit self-conscious. In fact, Rebecca was looking
at Jeffrey as if he were the only person in the
room.

"We're going to the Schooner Inn," Jeffrey
said, looking into Rebecca's violet eyes. "I've
made reservations. Barbara took a liking to
the place."

From the way Jeffrey was looking at Rebecca, he'd rather be going with *her*, Paul
thought. The attraction that Jeffrey felt was
so obvious on his face. What Miranda has been
telling me is true, he thought. She was right
all along. Does Barbara know? he wondered,
feeling a pang of sympathy for her.

Rebecca said good-bye and walked to the
other side of the store. Heads turned to follow
her as she passed. Each person that she
floated by gazed after her, their faces transformed by looks of wonder and astonishment.
A subtle thrill surged through the store, touching everyone inside.

Outside, Trent Marliss, Vicki Rorsch's boyfriend, tapped on the glass and waved. Paul waved back, thinking that Trent must not have seen Rebecca, or he'd have been on his way inside. When he turned back to Jeffrey, he noticed that he was still staring at Rebecca.

"Hey, Jeffrey, are you going to make up your mind about that necklace, or what?" Paul asked impatiently.

Jeffrey looked at Paul as if he had just come out of a dream. "Let's get out of here," he snapped. Stunned, Paul followed him from the store.

In the car, Jeffrey said nothing as he drove. It's Rebecca, Paul knew. That's the reason he looks so terrible. He wants Rebecca — and he feels guilty about Barbara. Paul thought of saying something about it, but one look at his friend's stony expression and tightly clenched jaw, and he decided against it.

They neared a minimarket, and Paul asked Jeffrey to stop for a moment. "I promised my mom I'd pick up some stuff for her card party tonight. Say — can I borrow your windbreaker for a minute while I go into the store? This weather is freaky. It's *cold* out there."

"Sure," said Jeffrey, looking distracted. He

removed his windbreaker and handed it to Paul.

"Be back in a minute," Paul said. He put on the jacket and headed into the store. Seeing Jeffrey so rattled disturbed him. Jeffrey had always been a rock, the one everyone looked up to.

Paul grabbed sodas, crackers, cheese, pretzels, and chips. As he stood in line, he told himself that Jeffrey would snap out of this. He'd realize that Barbara was the only one for him, and things would be the same between all of them as it was before.

Paul went to pay the clerk, and accidently reached into the pocket of Jeffrey's windbreaker. He felt something, and drew it out. He was holding the necklace that Jeffrey had admired in the store. The one he couldn't afford. The gold heart with a diamond chip.

Chapter 26

"It's impossible!" Jeffrey blurted out as Paul held up the necklace.

"It's *very* possible, Jeffrey. The necklace is right here in my hand. And I found it in the pocket of your jacket."

"I don't know how it ended up there," Jeffrey said. "You know me, Paul. I wouldn't steal it."

Paul looked at the shocked, agonized expression on his friend's face. Aloud, he said, "I know you wouldn't steal it, Jeffrey. But the necklace got into your pocket somehow. So *how*?"

Jeffrey slumped back against the seat of the car. His jaw was tensed and frown lines creased his forehead.

Outside, the fog was wafting through the air in an undulating, whisper-soft motion. It's like watching ghosts dancing in slow motion, Paul thought.

"I must have been distracted when I saw Rebecca," Jeffrey said after several moments. "I was holding the necklace, and that must have been when I put it in my pocket."

Distracted isn't the word, Paul thought. Jeffrey had looked overwhelmed and obsessed.

"What are you going to do about the necklace, Jeffrey? We could go right back to the store now, and explain everything to Mr. Stanton. If we do it right away, he'll understand that it was an honest mistake."

Paul was surprised to see Jeffrey shake his head *no*. "What's wrong?" he asked, stunned. "We can straighten this thing out right now, Jeffrey."

"*No*. I don't want to run into Rebecca again." Jeffrey jammed his hands into his pockets. That was a lie, he knew. He wanted to see Rebecca again, right now, more than he had ever wanted anything. He wanted to be with her so much that it made him afraid.

"You . . . *what?*" This is getting crazier by the minute, Paul thought. "She probably won't even be there now." Paul's words came out rapidly, tumbling over each other. "And anyway, what's the difference? It's not important. What *is* important is getting that necklace back to the store before Stanton starts thinking you stole it." Paul paused and waited for Jeffrey to say something. He didn't. "Come *on*, Jeffrey. Start making some sense," he said through gritted teeth.

But no matter what Paul said, Jeffrey stubbornly refused to go back to the store. Moments later, he dropped Paul off at his house, leaving him troubled and confused.

By the time Jeffrey got home, Mr. Stanton had already called the house. His employee had told him the necklace was missing.

"Mr. Stanton thought you might have some idea what happened to the necklace," Jeffrey's mother explained. Frowning, she asked, "Oh, my, you don't think one of the employees stole it, do you?"

Then Jeffrey had to tell his mother what had happened to the necklace. He left out the real reason he had not gone directly back to the store and returned it. "I took Paul around to a few places where he had errands to run, and by the time I found the necklace in my pocket it was so late. . . . Mom, I have to pick up Barbara soon."

Jeffrey's mother was looking at him with a strange, surprised expression.

"It's not an ordinary date, tonight. I'm taking Barbara out to dinner for her birthday. We have reservations."

Jeffrey wasn't used to lying, and he hated it. He didn't like having something to lie about. He liked hoping that he sounded convincing even less. So it was with a mixture of relief and remorse that he saw the awful, blank look of disbelief vanish from his mother's face.

"I understand. But you've got to call Mr. Stanton at the store and explain everything to him. Call right now. Don't wait until tomorrow."

"Of course!" Jeffrey said, with an emphasis he immediately thought sounded exaggerated. "I was planning to call him right away anyhow."

Immediately, Jeffrey looked up the number for Stanton's jewelry store in the telephone book. Had his mother really looked doubtful at first, or had he imagined it because he knew he wasn't telling the exact truth? he wondered.

A pit of nausea settled into his stomach as he dialed the number for the jewelry store. As he spoke to Mr. Stanton, he thought his words sounded hollow and rehearsed, as if he was reading them from cue cards.

Mr. Stanton made Jeffrey feel worse than ever. He told him that he understood perfectly what happened. Then he threw in a few jokes about Jeffrey having the talent to become a fine pickpocket.

By the time Jeffrey got off the phone, his forehead was coated with a film of perspiration. He went up to his room and closed the door. He put the necklace on the dresser.

I didn't take the necklace on purpose. Why do I feel so guilty? he asked himself.

Everything is fine, Jeffrey told himself yet again as he prepared to leave to pick up Barbara. Tomorrow, I'll return the necklace, and everything will be all right.

Then, just before he left the room, he slipped the necklace into his pocket.

Chapter 27

The evening was off to a bad start even before Jeffrey arrived at Barbara's house. With each moment that ticked by, the forces that had been set in motion by an unseen hand wove together tighter and tighter, into a trap for Jeffrey. As with quicksand, the more Jeffrey struggled, the worse off he became.

"Hi, Jeffrey," Barbara greeted him, answering the doorbell.

Jeffrey felt the same uncomfortable reaction he always had around her lately. Barbara was wearing a short, clinging black dress with a halter top. It's like something I've seen Rebecca wear, Jeffrey thought.

Barbara reached up and put her hand on the back of his neck. She kissed him lightly on the lips. Immediately, Jeffrey jerked away from her.

"What's the matter?" Barbara asked worriedly.

"Nothing," Jeffrey answered quickly. "It's just that you're wearing a different perfume, that's all."

"It's something new. Don't you like it?"

Jeffrey could see the hurt in Barbara's eyes. He kissed her forehead gently. How would I feel if Barbara were the one whose feelings had changed? he asked himself. He knew the answer. Miserable.

"I like the perfume very much," Jeffrey lied. "I just didn't expect it to be different."

"Oh, good." Barbara smiled.

As soon as they got in the car, Barbara unwittingly sent the wheel of fate spinning closer to disaster. "Jeffrey, can I have my present now?" she asked, her eyes dancing.

Jeffrey's heart sank. He had planned on telling Barbara that he wanted to give her the *perfect* present, and he just hadn't found it yet. When he had rehearsed the speech, he'd convinced himself that if he explained it that way, Barbara wouldn't be disappointed. Looking at her eager face, he knew he'd been kidding himself to ease his own conscience.

Jeffrey felt a stab of guilt. It wasn't fair to Barbara. He should have gotten her present a long time ago. She deserved to be happy on her birthday.

"I'm not giving you your present until we sit down to dinner at the restaurant," Jeffrey said, trying to make his voice sound light and teasing.

Barbara laughed. "Oh, all right. I can't wait to see what you picked out." Her voice was full of anticipation.

Jeffrey stared straight ahead at the road. Barbara loves the restaurant, he told himself. When she's having a romantic dinner, she won't mind having to wait for her present. I'll tell her then. He hoped that by some miracle, he was right.

"Reservation for Thomas," Jeffrey told the hostess as he and Barbara stepped into the Schooner's waiting area.

"Thomas." The woman smiled and looked down at her list. She tapped her pencil. "Thomas," she repeated, scanning the list a second time.

Jeffrey watched a wrinkle of concern pucker on Barbara's forehead. His heart flip-flopped. "I called a few days ago," he volunteered. The one thing I did right and *it's* going wrong, he thought desperately.

"I'm sorry," the woman said after checking the list a third time. There was genuine regret in her voice. "There must be some mix-up. I'm afraid your name isn't here."

"But I made the reservation," Jeffrey protested.

"I'm sure you did, and it's entirely our fault," replied the hostess. "But your name isn't here, and all of our tables are full. You can put your name on the waiting list if you like, but I don't think we'll be able to seat you for quite a while." She showed Jeffrey the waiting list, which contained over a dozen names.

"Look here," Jeffrey began angrily. Barbara tugged at his sleeve. "Jeffrey, don't make a scene. It's not that important. We'll just go someplace else." Barbara's voice sounded cheerful, but he could tell she was trying to conceal her true disappointment. It made him feel worse.

They left the restaurant and drove back toward Winthrop. "Let's just go to Sharkey's," Barbara said.

"No!" Jeffrey insisted, hating himself because he knew he was as involved with his own guilt as he was with ruining Barbara's evening. "We'll find a nice place to go."

And they did. But it didn't save the evening.

"Well, look who's here, it's Jeffrey and Barbara," Vicki exclaimed as the two of them entered Marano's, a small Italian restaurant in the heart of Winthrop. Marano's wasn't as fancy as the Schooner Inn, but it was cozy and romantic.

Vicki waved to Jeffrey and Barbara, and motioned them over to her table where she sat with Trent Marliss. "I thought you two were going to the Schooner Inn for Barbara's birthday," she cooed in honeyed tones.

"There was a mix-up with our reservations," Jeffrey said, trying to keep the edge out of his voice. "Hello, Trent."

"Happy birthday, Barbara," Trent said with a boyish grin. Trent was no rocket scientist, but he was a good-natured guy who had none of Vicki's sarcasm.

"It was my birthday two days ago. Look what my parents got me." Trent held up his wrist, displaying a Rolex watch. Jeffrey knew Trent's family was wealthy. He couldn't imagine spending so much money to know what time it was.

"Nice watch," Jeffrey said simply.

"It certainly is," Barbara agreed.

"My dad said he got it at Stanton's," Trent said. "The same place . . ." Suddenly, Trent fell silent.

What is the matter with him? Jeffrey wondered. He welcomed the chance to get away from the table. He hadn't enjoyed hearing Stanton's mentioned. It stirred up too many unpleasant thoughts.

"Well, nice talking to you. We're going to sit down and eat now." Jeffrey turned to walk away.

"Wait a second," Vicki said. "You remember I'm having a party next week, don't you? You're both coming, aren't you?" She paused for a moment and added, "Together?"

Jeffrey tensed as he heard Vicki's words. He hadn't known how strong his feelings were for Rebecca until recently, and he certainly hadn't thought anyone else had noticed. I might have known Vicki would have her radar out, he thought with disgust. But she shouldn't ruin Barbara's birthday with her catty games.

Before Jeffrey could think of anything to say, Barbara responded, "Of course, we'll be there."

Jeffrey glanced at Barbara sharply. Barbara was smiling openly at Vicki. She hadn't noticed the dig. "See you later, Vicki, Trent," Jeffrey said, steering Barbara away from the table.

"Bye." Barbara waved.

When they sat down at the table, Barbara said, "I don't mind not going to the Schooner

Inn. Really, Jeffrey, it's not important. I'm just happy to be here with you."

Jeffrey looked into Barbara's eyes. And then, he did something he'd been sure he'd never do. "Happy birthday, Barbara," he said, as he pulled the gold necklace from his pocket and put it in her hand.

Barbara's eyes widened in astonishment as she gazed at the necklace in her hand. "Oh, Jeffrey, it's so beautiful," she said. "I never dreamed of anything so special." She leaned across the table and kissed him.

As Barbara kissed him, Jeffrey stiffened. He realized where he had smelled that perfume before. Rebecca wore it — but not in real life. Rebecca wore it in a dream. The one where he had seen himself in his coffin.

Chapter 28

"It's a great party, Vicki. It doesn't matter about the weather. At least it's not so hot," said one of Vicki's party guests.

"Thanks," Vicki said. As she turned away, she grimaced. She had been hearing variations of the same statement ever since guests had begun arriving, and she was getting tired of it. She had wanted to have a party that was a *perfect event*, as her other parties had been.

Looking at the overcast sky and the steely gray cast on the water, Vicki sighed. Most of the days this summer had been hot — overwhelmingly so. Vicki had planned that everyone would be hurrying into the water for a quick swim, and then back to the air-conditioned party room she had rented. But it was much too cool to swim. She tugged at her sweatshirt. Now she couldn't even show off her new bathing suit.

"I don't like to swim anyway," someone beside her whispered.

Startled, Vicki whirled around. "Rebecca!" she exclaimed. "How did you know what I was thinking about?"

Rebecca laughed lightly. "I didn't. I saw you looking at the water and assumed your thoughts had something to do with swimming."

"Actually, I was thinking that I've got this great new bathing suit, and I'm stuck in this clunky sweatshirt and jeans." Vicki looked at Rebecca's outfit. She wore a clinging black tank top and matching black shorts. Everyone else had on sweaters or sweatshirts. "Aren't you cold?" Vicki asked.

"Not at all," Rebecca answered, smiling radiantly. "I love this weather."

"It's so gloomy," Vicki said. She looked over Rebecca's shoulder. "Oh, there're Jeffrey and Barbara." She was unable to suppress a sly smile. No sooner were the words out of her mouth than Jeffrey saw Rebecca and began heading over.

"Hello, Rebecca." Jeffrey looked deep into her eyes. There was no mistaking the look on his face.

My, my, my, it's worse than I thought, Vicki said to herself with a smirk. The rock of Gibraltar has cracked, and his heart is hanging out for all to see. And there's poor Barbara, completely oblivious.

"Aren't you going to say hello to *me*, Jeffrey?" Vicki said after a moment.

"Oh, hello, Vicki," Jeffrey murmured, looking distracted.

"Nice party," Barbara said, smiling.

She really doesn't suspect a thing, Vicki said to herself. Only Barbara could be so trusting and naive. "Barbara, would you help me with something?"

"Sure."

Jeffrey hadn't taken his eyes off Rebecca, and now the two of them were deep in conversation. He didn't even notice Barbara leave. *Somebody's* got to tell her, Vicki thought as they walked away. There was a smile of satisfaction on her lips.

Jeffrey wasn't able to savor his time alone with Rebecca for very long. Every guy at the party wanted to talk to her, to be near her.

And who can blame them? Jeffrey asked himself. He had never known anyone so completely captivating. It wasn't just Rebecca's beauty, enchanting though it was. It was Rebecca herself. Jeffrey was standing and staring at her when Paul approached.

"Hey, Jeffrey. I've got to talk to you."

Reluctantly, Jeffrey took his eyes off Rebecca. "Do we have to talk right now, Paul?"

Paul crossed his arms and looked steadily at Jeffrey. "What's the matter? Can't you leave Rebecca's side for a second? What I have to say is important. Hear me out, and you can get back to her."

Jeffrey was as surprised by Paul's hard tone of voice as he was by his words. He jammed his hands into his pockets. "What do you have to tell me?"

"Let's walk."

Together they walked to the edge of the water. Paul looked thoughtful.

"Jeffrey, something about you has changed. You're not the same person you used to be. Sometimes I feel like I don't even know you."

Paul was silent for a moment. He hoped that Jeffrey would say something, offer some explanation that would ease his mind. He didn't, so Paul went on.

"We've been friends for a long time, Jeffrey. So I'm going to tell you the truth. The way you've been panting after Rebecca lately, even when Barbara is around, is not nice to watch. Whatever Rebecca has done to you, it's not good."

Again, Paul stopped talking and waited for

Jeffrey to say something. When there was no response, he clenched and unclenched his fists in frustration.

"Come on, Jeffrey, what's going on? I feel like you're not even listening. Talk to me!"

Jeffrey opened his mouth to speak but, whatever he was going to say, Paul would never know, for just then Trent and Vicki came up, with Barbara. Paul noticed the distressed look on Barbara's face and the smug look Vicki was wearing.

"Hey, guys, having a good time?" Trent asked, smiling broadly.

Jeffrey nodded, and Paul answered, "Sure."

"I've been meaning to tell you, Jeffrey, that was a really cool move you made in the jewelry store. Through the window, I saw you lifting that necklace." Trent turned to Barbara. "Did you know your boyfriend stole your present?"

Everyone stood there in stunned silence. Barbara reached up and touched the necklace, an expression of surprise on her face. Without a word, she turned and ran away.

As she left, a look of embarrassment came over Trent's face.

"Trent, you're an idiot," Paul said.

Jeffrey was shaking with rage. "What you saw was an accident," he said. "I went back and paid for the necklace. Whatever made you tell that story to Barbara?"

A dull red blush had crept into Trent's complexion. "Believe me, Jeffrey," he stammered, "I can't explain it, but I didn't mean to say what I did. It was like somebody was moving my mouth for me, making me say the words. I just couldn't help it."

Barbara ran and ran. She couldn't believe that Jeffrey had stolen her necklace. But she was so upset and confused she didn't know what to believe anymore.

Barbara wanted to cry, but she held back the tears. If everyone knew there was something going on between Rebecca and Jeffrey, they would all know why she was crying, and feel sorry for her. Somehow she would control herself until she was alone at home.

Her whole world had turned upside down when Vicki told her that Jeffrey was after Rebecca. She'd tried to ignore the way he looked at her, and how much he talked about her. But she couldn't pretend anymore.

At the entrance to the ladies' room, Barbara stopped to catch her breath. Suddenly, she had a comforting thought. Rebecca wouldn't allow anything to happen between her and Jeffrey, Barbara told herself. After all, Rebecca was her friend. Somehow, she'd find a way to talk to Rebecca about the situation.

Taking a deep breath, Barbara entered the ladies' room. There was Rebecca, standing before the mirror. She was brushing her long black hair. "Why, Barbara, you look as if you've seen a ghost," Rebecca said.

"Maybe I just need some makeup," Barbara said nervously. Every time she saw Rebecca, she was amazed all over again at how extraordinarily beautiful she was. Now that she stood next to her, Barbara felt awkward. What would she say? Have you and my boyfriend been seeing each other behind my back? If he came after you, you wouldn't let anything happen, would you? Everything seemed so lame — or worse, insulting. There had to be a way to start the conversation.

Barbara decided to begin by talking about something else. She searched for a topic. She'd always found it easy to talk to Rebecca before. Now it was different.

Then Barbara looked at Rebecca's choker. She always wore it around her neck, and yet Barbara had never really looked at it before. It was really quite unusual.

"That's a beautiful choker, Rebecca," Barbara remarked.

Rebecca flashed one of her dazzling smiles.

"Thank you. I've had it for a long time."

"I've never seen one quite like it." Then Barbara reached up to touch the black velvet choker that encircled Rebecca's throat.

Suddenly, Rebecca reached up and pushed Barbara's hand away. She turned on her, eyes blazing. "Don't you dare touch that!" she shrieked, her voice full of fury. "I never let anyone touch my necklace!"

Barbara backed away from her. She had never seen Rebecca, or anyone, so enraged. It seemed insane, but she thought Rebecca looked mad enough to *kill* her.

For just an instant, Barbara saw Rebecca's eyes flash with a burning red color. For just a moment, Rebecca was transformed into something that wasn't even human.

Chapter 29

Terrified, Barbara backed away from Rebecca. Then she turned and ran from the ladies' room, colliding with Jeffrey just outside the door.

"Barbara, I've been looking all over for you," Jeffrey said anxiously. He looked into her eyes. "The necklace is paid for, Barbara. I didn't steal it."

Her voice shaking, Barbara grabbed Jeffrey's arm and said, "Jeffrey, let's get away from here, please. I want to get away from here right now."

Jeffrey looked at Barbara's pale face and terrified expression. "What's the matter?"

Pulling Jeffrey by the hand, Barbara hurried along. "I can't talk about it now. It's too . . . terrible. But I have to talk to you alone." Barbara looked at Jeffrey with wide frightened eyes. "Can we go out on the boat together?"

Barbara was referring to the little cabin

cruiser Jeffrey's father kept at the nearby marina. Jeffrey hesitated. "It's not such a nice day. Are you sure that's what you want to do?"

"Yes," Barbara said emphatically, holding Jeffrey's hand tightly. "I want us to be alone."

"Well, all right then. I'll just stop and tell Vicki we're going."

"No!" Barbara snapped. "Let's just go."

Jeffrey couldn't imagine what had happened to make Barbara look so terrified and upset. "All right, all right, we'll just go," he agreed. Together they hurried down the beach toward the marina.

While Jeffrey untied the boat and prepared to get underway, Barbara kept looking around nervously. Several times, she urged him to hurry. Growing more and more alarmed, Jeffrey did everything as fast as he could.

Jeffrey started the motor. They headed away from the dock. Silently, Jeffrey steered the boat, waiting for Barbara to tell him what had happened. Instead, she was quiet.

Jeffrey drove the boat out into the bay. Still, Barbara said nothing. Whatever had taken place must have been awfully frightening, Jeffrey thought. Barbara's expression was still as terrified as when she'd first asked him to take the boat out. But they'd been on the water for nearly fifteen minutes, and she hadn't said a word.

Finally, Jeffrey could take it no longer. "You've got to tell me what happened, Barbara. No matter how hard it is."

"I can't, Jeffrey," Barbara gasped. "I feel awful. I'm so sick." Barbara clutched at her stomach. "I'm going below deck to lie down," she said weakly.

"Take it easy," Jeffrey said. "I'm going to turn the boat around and head for the dock. I'll take you to the doctor." He was frightened and nervous.

"I love you, Jeffrey," Barbara whispered. Then she went below.

Anguish tore through Jeffrey's heart as he watched her go. How could he bear to hurt her? Feelings of guilt overwhelmed him.

But Jeffrey soon realized that there was no time to think of that now. Something was happening that took his mind off his tortured feelings. The sky was darkening rapidly, filling up with ominous gray clouds. The sea was growing rougher. A storm was brewing.

The boat began to pitch and roll. Jeffrey began to fear that he wouldn't make it back to land before the storm blew up. He didn't like the angry look of those waves.

"Jeffrey . . ."

At the sound of the voice, Jeffrey was shot through with a combination of amazement and delight. There was no mistaking whose voice it was. "Rebecca," he breathed.

Jeffrey turned to look at her. Hungrily, his eyes devoured the image before him. Her raven hair blew back in the wind, the waves wilder than those of the sea. She glowed with a fire of her own. Her eyes burned into his.

"I heard you talking about going out on the boat." Rebecca came toward him, looking at him the way he'd often dreamed of, yearned for. As her slender hand touched the side of his face, Jeffrey was speechless. His heart ached with love.

"I couldn't stand to be away from you," Rebecca said, gazing deep into his eyes.

Jeffrey took her hand in his, and placed it over his heart. "You don't know how I've longed for you," he said softly.

Rebecca leaned close to him, and whispered into his ear. "I want you to remember something," she said. "No matter what happens, I'll always stand by you. Your friends will turn against you, but I'll always be there. And in the end, I'll be the only one you can turn to. You'll see . . ."

Jeffrey listened in astonishment to her words. She was looking at him with an expression of absolute confidence, as if she had no doubt of her ability to foretell the future.

Jeffrey started to ask Rebecca the meaning of her words, but the question died on his lips. The boat pitched forward in the choppy water. As Jeffrey struggled to keep his balance, he saw Rebecca standing, calm and still.

As he stared, Rebecca slowly began to fade before Jeffrey's eyes. In moments, she vanished completely.

Chapter 30

"Rebecca!" Jeffrey gasped incredulously as her face reappeared before him. She was so close that he saw the golden flecks in her violet eyes. When she spoke, she leaned closer still.

"I was so worried about you," she said softly. "The boat lurched, and you fell and hit your head. You were knocked unconscious."

Jeffrey looked up at her. She was cradling his head in her arms. He thought she looked like an angel. He reached up and touched her face gently. His fingers brushed her ruby lips.

"I'm all right now," Jeffrey said in a hushed voice. "So long as you're here with me, I'll be all right."

At that moment, Jeffrey knew his words were true. Whatever happened, he wanted only this — to be with Rebecca as he was right now, knowing that she cared for him. Nothing else mattered.

Rebecca took Jeffrey's hand and stood up slowly. Jeffrey got to his feet, still looking deeply into her eyes. "I love you, Rebecca," he said, with all the feeling in his heart. "I love you more than I've ever loved anyone. More than I thought was possible."

He put his arms around Rebecca and drew her close. The night and the storm slipped away as he felt the softness of her lips on his.

As they kissed, Jeffrey felt his heart soar. His soul expanded and grew full of light.

Jeffrey stroked Rebecca's silken hair. Her soft hands touched his face. Together, they looked out into the night.

The fog was wafting over the sea like smoke. Moonlight suddenly appeared and illuminated the storm-tossed ocean with an eerie glow.

Rebecca turned to Jeffrey, her face wreathed in a halo of light. "This is for you," she said, and pressed something into his hand.

Jeffrey looked down to see what it was, and his mind exploded in a flash of shock and disbelief. He and Rebecca were no longer on the boat. They were standing in the air above the water.

He looked at Rebecca in amazement. Then

suddenly, Jeffrey was overcome with a horrible, smothering fear. He was falling, falling, away from Rebecca. From above, Rebecca smiled down as the water engulfed him. Helplessly, he saw the surface of the ocean closing over his head. Then he couldn't see anything anymore.

Jeffrey sank deeper and deeper into the murky water. It was as if there were weights on his feet, pulling him down and down. He thrashed his arms and legs helplessly. His lungs screamed for air, and he was overcome with terror.

Then suddenly, everything changed. Jeffrey felt himself break free of the water. He was lying somewhere, surrounded by a curtain of darkness. His terror ebbed away like the tide, and he felt calm and peaceful. There was silence all around.

Jeffrey realized that he wasn't breathing, but it didn't matter anymore. There was no need to breathe.

No need to breathe. Jeffrey's mind felt so fuzzy, he was only able to think with great effort. Ever so slowly, he turned the thought over and over in his mind. *There was no need to breathe.*

Then Jeffrey was consumed by a horror infinitely worse than before. He tried to move, but even the flicker of an eyelid was impossible. For an instant, he thought he was paralyzed.

Then he realized he was dead.

Chapter 31

Jeffrey shook his head back and forth and blinked several times. There was darkness and silence all around. It was like being in a coffin.

Jeffrey screamed, a hollow, anguished sound. As he screamed, the dream came flooding back to him. It was just like all the rest, ending with him dead, in his coffin. But it was just a dream, he told himself. Just a dream.

His breath was coming in short, raspy bursts. For several moments he had no idea where he was. Gradually, his breathing grew more regular, and he realized that he was lying on a cold, hard floor. He was soaking wet, and the floor was wet, too. It moved, and Jeffrey slid helplessly across it.

I'm on the boat, he realized. He sat up and put his face in his hands. His head hurt terribly, and his thoughts were muddled and confused. Nothing made any sense. The last thing he remembered was that he'd been talking to Rebecca, and then something had happened.

I must have blacked out, he decided. While I was unconscious, I had one of those horrible dreams.

He recalled that Rebecca had given him something in the dream. He asked himself what it was.

Jeffrey's thoughts were cut short as another violent motion of the boat sent him sliding once more. He hit something he couldn't see, and grunted in pain. Groping blindly, he found the railing and pulled himself to his feet. Holding on tight, he peered out into the darkness. The sight before him made his heart race in his chest.

Fog blanketed the ocean, making it impossible to see more than a few feet ahead. But Jeffrey could tell that the waves rocking the boat were huge. As he stood there, struggling to keep from losing his grip on the cold, slippery railing, a wave came crashing over the side of the boat and knocked him down.

Somehow, Jeffrey managed to grab the railing again and get to his feet. The boat tumbled wildly through the waves.

When Jeffrey regained his balance, he saw that the wheel was whirling madly around. Holding onto the railing he pulled himself around until he was near, then stumbled toward it. He reached out and caught it as it spun around.

The boat was thrown up in the air by a wave. It came down with a vicious *thwack!* against the water.

Jeffrey willed his presence of mind to return. He couldn't afford to panic. Rebecca and Barbara were depending on him. He assumed that they were safely below deck, and he prayed he could get them all out of this unharmed.

Struggling to stay on his feet, Jeffrey gripped the wheel of the boat. He forced his mind to ignore the fear he felt and focus on what he had to do. Since he had no idea where he was, the only thing he could do was to try to stay afloat. The thought of being pulled far out to sea chilled his heart.

Grasping the slippery steering wheel, Jeffrey fought to keep the boat from capsizing. He tried his best to turn the wheel to steer the boat so that it could best ride the waves. It took all his strength as the ocean tossed the little boat around.

As the night wore on, Jeffrey grew weary and bone-tired. His muscles ached, even his brain felt like a weight. When he thought he could take it no longer, he gritted his teeth and held on.

After what seemed like hours, the sea began to calm down. Its angry thrashing gradually subsided until the waves no longer lashed at the boat, but rocked it gently.

In the dark water surrounded by fog, Jeffrey felt as if he were all alone in some strange, shrouded patch of the world. Too numb with exhaustion to feel relief, he decided it was safe to let go of the wheel and radio for help.

Moments later, Jeffrey's heart sank. The radio was dead.

Jeffrey did the only thing left to do. He sent up a flare. But he didn't have much hope that anyone would see it.

He dared not think of how the situation would look in the sunlight. If, with the help of the compass and maps, he could figure out where they were, he hoped they had enough gasoline to make it to shore.

Jeffrey sent another flare blazing into the fog. He watched it burn, and then slowly turned to go below deck and check on Rebecca and Barbara. As he stumbled toward the ladder, he reproached himself for thinking of Rebecca first.

Suddenly, he heard a horn in the distance. Jeffrey wheeled around, picked up a flare, and sent it flashing into the night. Then he signalled with his own horn, three short blasts, three long, and three more short, for SOS.

The foghorn on the other boat signalled back.

After several minutes of signalling back and forth, Jeffrey could see the form of a boat dimly through the fog as it headed toward him. "This is the US Coast Guard," someone called to him through a bullhorn. "Prepare for us to come alongside."

Prepare, thought Jeffrey. It's all I can do to stand up.

Moments later, two men boarded the cabin cruiser. They were dressed in slickers bearing the Coast Guard insignia, and hip waders. They introduced themselves as Foster and Garrod.

"I'm very glad to see you," Jeffrey told them, a tide of relief washing through him.

"You're lucky to be alive, my friend," Foster said. "It wouldn't take much for a boat to capsize in that storm."

"It blew up so suddenly," Jeffrey said. "I was trying to keep the boat afloat, and then I guess I hit my head. I blacked out. When I came to, I was afraid we'd drifted out to sea."

"Not a very comforting thought," Foster shook his head. "Don't worry, we'll get you out of here. We're going to attach a towline to your boat and pull you ashore."

Jeffrey nodded. Suddenly, he felt he was going to collapse. "What time is it?" he asked, weakly.

Foster looked at his watch. "About eleven-thirty," he said.

"Eleven-thirty," Jeffrey echoed in amazement. "We left the dock in the afternoon!"

Foster's eyes narrowed. "That's a surprise. You didn't drift very far at all." He stroked the gray stubble on his chin thoughtfully. "It's strange."

Jeffrey was about to mention Rebecca and Barbara, when Foster's partner, Garrod, came up from below deck. He was carrying Barbara's purse. "I found this," he said, dangling it by the shoulder strap.

Jeffrey recognized the purse right away. "Is Barbara all right?" he blurted out. "Did you talk to Rebecca?"

Immediately, Jeffrey knew his greater concern was for Rebecca. It made him feel ashamed.

Then Jeffrey realized that Garrod was staring at him strangely. "I found the purse. But there's nobody else on this boat."

Chapter 32

Completely exhausted, Jeffrey sat with a blanket draped around his shoulders. He had been at the police station for over two hours now. They had brought him to this dingy office and questioned him continuously. By now, he could probably hear the questions in his sleep. If only he could get some sleep. He was so very, very tired.

"Something just isn't adding up," Detective Radler said, pacing back and forth in front of Jeffrey. "Let's go over this again."

"We've been over it again and again!" Jeffrey exploded. "I don't know what happened to Barbara. We went out on the boat. Barbara said she was sick, and went below deck to lie down. That's the last I saw of her."

The detective leaned his face close to Jeffrey's. Jeffrey could see the pores in his skin, and the red, broken blood vessels in his eyes.

He could smell him, too. A mixture of tobacco and sweat.

"Now you listen here, young man. You're in a lot of trouble, and the more you keep trying to be slick, the deeper in you get."

"I'm not trying to be slick," Jeffrey said angrily, looking the detective in the eye. "Why don't you ask Rebecca? She was on the boat."

"So you said." A strange smile spread across Detective Radler's face. "But now that we've checked into it, it turns out that you're lying. A couple of friends of yours came by here when they couldn't find you. We asked them some questions. They said you spent a lot of time at the party talking to a girl named Rebecca Webster. But Rebecca stayed until the party was over."

Detective Radler stood up and looked down at Jeffrey. "You said you took the boat out in the afternoon. How could this Rebecca have been on the boat with you, when everyone else says she was there at the party until after dark?" He slammed his palm hard on the table.

"But that's impossible," Jeffrey protested. "They're mistaken. You've got to talk to Rebecca. She'll tell you what happened."

"Well, it so happens," the detective said, "we've got a problem there. We can't find Rebecca. She's gone."

One of the Coast Guard staff came in and handed the detective a note. "Excuse me a minute," he said to Jeffrey. "Don't go away," he added, snidely.

Jeffrey watched as Detective Radler went to the outer office and dialed a telephone. Jeffrey could see him, nodding as he listened to the voice at the other end of the line. His face was expressionless.

In a few moments, the detective returned. "It looks like you're in a lot more trouble than you thought, son. It seems your girlfriend Barbara's body just washed up on the beach. From the marks on her neck, it looks like she's been strangled."

"No!" Jeffrey burst out, overcome with shock and grief.

The detective cocked his head toward Jeffrey, looking at him with a puzzled expression. "What's that you've got in your hands? You've been twisting something the whole time you've been sitting here."

Jeffrey looked down absently. He had been so nervous, he hadn't even noticed what he'd been doing with his hands. Now he saw that he was twisting a black velvet ribbon, much like the one Rebecca wore around her neck.

Suddenly he found the lost memory he had been seeking. It flashed into his brain with piercing, crystal clarity. This was the ribbon from Rebecca's choker. When they were on the boat, she had pulled it off her neck. It tore, and the jewel came loose. She had put the piece of ribbon in his hand.

Jeffrey jumped to his feet. He held the piece of ribbon out in front of him. "This belongs to Rebecca!" he said. "It's part of her choker necklace. It proves she was on the boat. While we were on the water, she gave it to me . . ."

Jeffrey's voice trailed off suddenly. He realized that he had been about to say, *in a dream*. He looked at the black velvet ribbon, unable to believe his eyes. Rebecca had given him the ribbon *in a dream*.

Jeffrey rubbed a hand across his forehead, and sat down. His thoughts were whirling in his head. When he looked up he saw Detective Radler looking at him piercingly.

"It won't do you any good to make up any more stories. Won't do you any good to try to act crazy, either. You just might as well tell me that you killed that girl and threw her overboard. Because I know you did."

Jeffrey slumped in the chair. What really happened on the boat? he wondered. How could Barbara be dead? And where, oh where, was Rebecca?

His mind was a tangle of confusion. He had

seen Rebecca on the boat, but he'd had a dream about her, too. A sick feeling of fear spread through him. It was impossible to tell what was real and what was a dream. He looked at Detective Radler's smirking face, and wondered — what if I *really am* going crazy?

Chapter 33

It had been two weeks since Barbara's body had washed up on the beach.

After questioning him for hours, Detective Radler still had only suspicions. With no evidence strong enough to hold him, he had let Jeffrey go home.

But Detective Radler had gone to great lengths to let Jeffrey know that he was still a suspect, and the detective would be watching. He'd gone so far as to tell Jeffrey he thought he was guilty, and he intended to make it his job to prove it.

In the two weeks following Barbara's death, Radler showed he was as good as his word. He'd interviewed everyone who was at the party, all of Jeffrey's close friends, and even his acquaintances.

The detective stopped by Jeffrey's house occasionally, to ask Jeffrey a few more questions. Jeffrey thought he just wanted to needle him to see if he'd crack. Detective Radler delighted in keeping Jeffrey informed of the progress of his investigation.

The fact that everyone at the party had seen Rebecca on shore, when Jeffrey claimed she was on the boat, was especially damaging. With Rebecca nowhere to be found, everything pointed to the fact that he had been caught in a lie.

When the lie was put together with the talk of Jeffrey and Barbara's failing romance, and the numerous stories of Jeffrey's stranger and stranger behavior of late, things looked even worse. And, of course, there was the black velvet ribbon.

"If I strangled Barbara with the ribbon, would I be stupid enough to have it in my hands while I was being questioned?" Jeffrey asked Detective Radler over and over again. But the detective wasn't swayed in the least. He kept saying Jeffrey thought he was a sly, clever fellow, but he'd find out he wasn't so smart after all.

Paul had come over a couple of days after the accident. Jeffrey told him the same story he told the detective.

As long as he lived, Jeffrey would never, never forget the look of disbelief on Paul's face. And he would never forget his own terrible feeling of disappointment and betrayal when he saw it.

Paul, sitting in a chair in Jeffrey's bedroom, raked his hands through his black hair and stared at Jeffrey in silence. "About Rebecca," he said, finally. "Everybody saw her at the party, so you must be lying. I won't let myself think of why you'd lie, Jeffrey. Not after what happened to Barbara."

Paul was Jeffrey's best friend. If anyone would believe him, Paul would. But when Jeffrey could think of nothing to say, Paul had left without a word. They hadn't spoken since.

After that, the few times Jeffrey had left the house, he saw the accusing looks on the faces of the people who had been his friends. Overnight, every one of them had turned against him. Rebecca's prophecy had come to pass, and yet she was not around for Jeffrey to turn to.

Meanwhile, Jeffrey thought of nothing but Rebecca. He spent hours alone in his room, while visions of her filled his brain.

The visions gave Jeffrey no comfort. Day after day passed with no sign of Rebecca. Her absence made him long for her all the more. He was tortured with remorse that he thought of Rebecca, and yet Barbara had died and he scarcely thought of her at all.

Jeffrey's friends waited for him to reappear as the Jeffrey they had known, strong and unafraid. The old Jeffrey would never have stopped trying to convince them his story was true. But Jeffrey was not the same. The way he had withdrawn into himself served to make everyone more suspicious than ever.

At first, Jeffrey had gone to Rebecca's house on the cliffs every day, searching for her. The place brought back memories of being there with her, her face lit by candlelight, or radiant in the sun. But now the house looked more deserted than ever. There was no sign of life.

After having hopes of seeing Rebecca dashed again and again, Jeffrey vowed one day not to return. The pain was too great. Jeffrey thought, Rebecca has abandoned me. For the first time in his life, he felt despair so great that it was more than he could bear. He had to forget about Rebecca.

But as the days went by, one after the other, Jeffrey was unable to banish Rebecca from his thoughts for even an instant. He awoke one night from a dream where he had seen Rebecca wandering in the woods, her whole being glowing in the moonlight. She had called his name.

Jeffrey peered out his window into the night. Fog swirled in the darkness. There was a full moon in the sky, just as there had been in his dream. Then Jeffrey knew he couldn't stop himself from going to her house on the cliffs one last time.

As he drove to Rebecca's house, Jeffrey felt breathless with expectation. He told himself to face the fact that Rebecca would not be there, just as she hadn't been the other times. Time and time again, he told himself to go home. But he knew it was useless. He would try to see Rebecca that night, and he would try again and again for as long as he lived.

And then Jeffrey reached the rusty iron gate that stood in front of Rebecca's house. His heart pounding, Jeffrey got out of the car and started up the walk.

The full moon glittered through the bare branches, making the fog glow with a pale, eerie light. The windows in the house were dark. They stared back at him, gaping, as if mocking his love and his hope.

There is no one here, Jeffrey thought. His hopes plummeted. He felt a sorrow so deep that he thought his heart would break.

He asked himself how one human being could cause such longing, such despair. He told himself that it wasn't reasonable — but he knew he was beyond reason.

Jeffrey willed himself to get in his car and leave the place, and never come back. But he could not move. At least if he was near Rebecca's house, he was near her, too, in a way. And then he saw her.

"Rebecca!"

At first, he thought she was an hallucination, for Rebecca looked more like a spirit than a creature of this earth. Her whole being was lit up by moonlight. She floated toward him over the ground, her filmy black dress flowing around her body.

"Jeffrey," she called to him. "Jeffrey, I told you that they would turn against you. That I would be the only one you could turn to."

"Yes," Jeffrey breathed. He prayed that he was not dreaming. "Rebecca," he said, holding out his arms to her.

And then, fulfilling Jeffrey's deepest desire, Rebecca held out her arms, reaching for him.

They embaced, and Jeffrey kissed Rebecca passionately, entwining her in his arms.

The world fell away as he kissed Rebecca. He heard a rush of wind in his ears, and felt his heart leaping in his chest. All his senses were filled with the wonder of her. For the first time since the accident, he felt alive.

Jeffrey tangled his fingers in the silken masses of her black hair. He pulled gently away from her and looked into her eyes, losing himself in their violet shadows.

Rebecca stroked the side of Jeffrey's face, and looked into his eyes lovingly. "You have been very sad, haven't you?" she asked. The fog swirled around them.

"It's been unbearable. I don't know what's happening to me. My whole life is falling down around me, and there's nothing I can do to stop it. All I know is that I've longed for you, and I can't live without you."

As Rebecca looked into Jeffrey's eyes, he saw her expression change slowly. It was as if a curtain of darkness had fallen over her face. Jeffrey stared back at her, the love of all his heart, and tried to comprehend what was happening.

Then in a single, violent motion, Rebecca, once again wearing the choker, tore it from her neck and threw it on the ground. The velvet ribbon had covered a hideous, twisted scar.

For a moment Jeffrey was so shocked, he was unable to make a sound. Then he gasped, "Rebecca." He wanted to turn his head away from the terrible sight, but he was unable to take his eyes off the ghastly scar.

"What happened to you, Rebecca? Who did this to you? Why?" Jeffrey said in an anguished voice.

Rebecca gazed steadily at Jeffrey, taking in the horrified expression on his face. "I, too, know what it is to be falsely accused," she said, her voice low and mysterious. "You think that you have known betrayal and despair, but it's *nothing* compared to what I have endured."

Jeffrey saw icy coldness in the eyes that only moments before had looked at him lovingly. What, oh what, had gone wrong, he wondered, frantically.

Rebecca's face twisted into a mask of rage. "I've waited a long, long, time for my revenge. Now my plan is finally coming true, and my soul will have some peace."

Rebecca pulled away from Jeffrey's arms. She saw the deep sadness on his face, and her lips curved in a smile of wicked satisfaction.

"I know you love me, Jeffrey. Your love for me is so great that it's almost more than you can bear. And now I'm leaving you, and your love will torture and torment you."

Jeffrey watched Rebecca turn and walk away, floating through the mist. A horrible feeling of emptiness overcame him. Inside, he felt something break and die.

"Jeffrey," Rebecca called back to him through the swirling mists. "My nightmare is almost over. But yours is just beginning."

How will Rebecca carry out her frightening promise of revenge? Why does she want to torment Jeffrey? Read the next Dark Moon: Dreams of Revenge.

THRILLERS

D.E. Atkins
- ❏ MC45246-0 Mirror, Mirror — $3.25
- ❏ MC45349-1 The Ripper — $3.25
- ❏ MC44941-9 Sister Dearest — $2.95

A. Bates
- ❏ MC45829-9 The Dead Game — $3.25
- ❏ MC43291-5 Final Exam — $3.25
- ❏ MC44582-0 Mother's Helper — $3.50
- ❏ MC44238-4 Party Line — $3.25

Caroline B. Cooney
- ❏ MC44316-X The Cheerleader — $3.25
- ❏ MC41641-3 The Fire — $3.25
- ❏ MC43806-9 The Fog — $3.25
- ❏ MC45681-4 Freeze Tag — $3.25
- ❏ MC45402-1 The Perfume — $3.25
- ❏ MC44884-6 The Return of the Vampire — $2.95
- ❏ MC41640-5 The Snow — $3.25
- ❏ MC45680-6 The Stranger — $3.50
- ❏ MC45682-2 The Vampire's Promise — $3.50

Richie Tankersley Cusick
- ❏ MC43115-3 April Fools — $3.25
- ❏ MC43203-6 The Lifeguard — $3.25
- ❏ MC43114-5 Teacher's Pet — $3.25
- ❏ MC44235-X Trick or Treat — $3.25

Carol Ellis
- ❏ MC46411-6 Camp Fear — $3.25
- ❏ MC44768-8 My Secret Admirer — $3.25
- ❏ MC47101-5 Silent Witness — $3.25
- ❏ MC46044-7 The Stepdaughter — $3.25
- ❏ MC44916-8 The Window — $2.95

Lael Littke
- ❏ MC44237-6 Prom Dress — $3.25

Jane McFann
- ❏ MC46690-9 Be Mine — $3.25

Christopher Pike
- ❏ MC43014-9 Slumber Party — $3.50
- ❏ MC44256-2 Weekend — $3.50

Edited by T. Pines
- ❏ MC45256-8 Thirteen — $3.50

Sinclair Smith
- ❏ MC45063-8 The Waitress — $2.95

Barbara Steiner
- ❏ MC46425-6 The Phantom — $3.50

Robert Westall
- ❏ MC41693-6 Ghost Abbey — $3.25
- ❏ MC43761-5 The Promise — $3.25
- ❏ MC45176-6 Yaxley's Cat — $3.25

Available wherever you buy books, or use this order form.

Scholastic Inc., P.O. Box 7502, 2931 East McCarty Street, Jefferson City, MO 65102

Please send me the books I have checked above. I am enclosing $_____ (please add $2.00 to cover shipping and handling). Send check or money order — no cash or C.O.D.s please.

Name _____ Age _____

Address_____

City_____ State/Zip_____

Please allow four to six weeks for delivery. Offer good in the U.S. only. Sorry, mail orders are not available to residents of Canada. Prices subject to change.   T294

THRILLERS